LUCÍA ASHTA

SMOKY MOUNTAIN PACK

FORGED WOLF

FORGED WOLF

SMOKY MOUNTAIN PACK BOOK ONE

LUCÍA ASHTA

Forged Wolf

Smoky Mountain Pack ~ Book One

Copyright © 2021 by Lucía Ashta

www.LuciaAshta.com

All rights reserved. No part of this book may be reproduced in any form or by any electronic or mechanical means, including information storage and retrieval systems, without written permission from the author, except for the use of brief quotations in a book review.

This is a work of fiction. Any resemblance to actual persons, places, or events is purely coincidental.

Cover design by Mirela Barbu

Editing by Ocean's Edge Editing

Proofreading by Geesey Editorial Services

*For the wild magic inside all of us.
Let loose the powerful mofo that you are!
Rawwwwr.*

*And also for Leia Stone.
Thank you for being a wonderful friend,
who always has my back.
Love you, girl.*

Own your badassery.

ZASHA VOLKOV

FORGED WOLF

CHAPTER ONE

ZASHA

HER PAPA WAS her whole world for as long as she could remember, since her mother left them when she was a young girl, sneaking out in the middle of the night, never to return. All the woman left behind were some serious abandonment issues and distorted memories of her fake laugh and chintzy perfume. Whether they were real or not, Zasha had no idea. Nothing much about her mother seemed real. She was a ghost, and it had taken most of Zasha's life to learn not to hate her.

Zasha Volkov predicted the day her papa died would be the worst of her life. She anticipated the soul-crushing weight that didn't let her breathe, that made her wonder whether she'd ever be able to feel anything other than this heart-battering pain.

She'd expected to stumble when he died, and

she'd been preparing for the moment of his passing for years. She'd observed him as he rubbed at his chest when he thought she wasn't looking, trying to ease the pain that never fully left him. It was his heart that finally killed him. And no, he didn't succumb to a heart attack like the doctors said. A broken heart killed him. He died because of a woman who never deserved him.

Zasha fought the writing on the wall for a long time. She spent her savings on consultations with medical experts her father refused to see until she begged him to go, and once he did he grumbled the entire time. He was old school from an old world. His life had been hard since the moment he came into it. It's how he left it too.

But none of that was surprising. She knew her papa better than anyone.

What did surprise Zasha was that the day she anticipated would be the worst of her life could somehow be even more horrible than she'd imagined.

When her father drew his last breath, no longer suffering as his heart squeezed the last drop of life from him, she broke. Really, she shattered into a million fragments she'd be lucky to ever piece back together.

And Zasha Volkov wasn't lucky. Never had been. Like her papa, she'd lived a hard life in a hard city where the easy breaks always happened to other people.

Her papa had a crew of friends who were like brothers. They'd been at the hospital with her, where she'd dragged her father despite his protests—though he'd refused an ambulance, saying they'd never finish paying off the bill.

Her papa's friends had been more life partners to him than the wife he never replaced. Big, stalwart brutes of men, they were her family. They stayed in the hospital with her all night while doctors and nurses tried to save her father's life. When they failed, her papa's friends—*brothers*—thumped Zasha awkwardly on the back and spoke rough words of comfort into her hair, calling her *volchok* as her father had done. They sniffled, but didn't let a tear wrench free. They were hard men who didn't cry; crying never solved a damn thing.

When Zasha couldn't take it anymore, when she needed to scream and rage at the injustices of life, they stayed at the hospital with her papa's body.

But when she left the hospital a while before dawn, she didn't yell or punch something as she thought she would. She didn't even cry as she feared she would. Inside, it was dark, eerily silent, and devastatingly cold, like she'd never warm up again. Before dawn broke, Zasha allowed herself to sink into weakness as she walked the mostly abandoned streets of Flaming Arrow. At that hour, those who still occupied the streets were mostly passed out after a night of desperate indulgence. Flaming Arrow was a city that only the hopeless remained in for long. Anyone with a chance at a better life fled the city sooner or later.

Like her mother had, when she'd latched on to a man who wasn't her husband, seeing him as her opportunity for salvation and citizenship status.

As Zasha passed dark alleys punctuated by the stench of urine, she hunched into her oversized hoodie and wondered what she'd do now. Her papa had tried to convince her to flee Flaming Arrow dozens of times, maybe hundreds. But she refused to abandon him, and he wouldn't quit the city that had become a home to him despite its often unkind treatment. He wouldn't leave his brothers or their families. Their bond was deeper than blood. They had each others' backs in a world that didn't mind whether they lived or died.

Zasha didn't want to leave her uncles any more than she did the memories of her papa that would linger in this place. She had no idea yet how she'd move on without her father and his constant strength, to start all over in an unfamiliar city, where no one would know her and no one would care. Still, it might be the only way she'd make it past the emptiness inside that was eating away at her will to live like acid on metal.

"Dammit, Papa," Zasha moaned aloud.

The weakness that rang through her shook her to her core. It was the one thing she was never supposed to reveal. *Never*. Papa and her uncles had pounded the understanding into her: *Predators prey on weakness*. They knew. They'd fled the deep mountains of Eastern Europe. When they'd opposed the local mafia, they'd been hunted, so they'd taken the women they wanted to marry and begin families with, and they'd left their birthplace behind.

Zasha was a petite woman, but her papa and her uncles had taught her to fight, and she was damn good at it. Once she turned eighteen, she made her living cage fighting and kickboxing in the ring. Since she was a young girl, her family taught her the importance of always carrying herself with strength. *The vibe you put off wins half your fights for you*, they'd say in their thick Eastern European accents. At all of five feet and one-half inch, she'd had to become tougher than those larger than her to hold her own. She'd learned to surprise her opponents and dominate in the cage and ring, and when her challengers knew of her reputation, she moved faster and with more agility than they, winning more times than not.

She couldn't afford to lose, because when she did, the knockouts were brutal. Scrappy and determined, she practiced harder than everyone else so she could come out on top.

So when she was attacked from behind, even though the assault surprised her, she should have been able to give her assailants the shock of their lives. She should have spun on them and punished them for taking advantage of the vulnerable.

She didn't. Fully absorbed by her grief, her reactions lagged. Muscle memory delayed by seconds before it kicked in. Not only must her attackers have singled her out because she was so evidently broken, but they didn't play by any kind of rules despite their already significant advantage in bulk and numbers.

Never drop your guard, her papa had told her perhaps a thousand times. Then he'd gone and died and his words echoed dully through her as one of her attackers grabbed her from behind.

He wrapped strong arms around her torso, pinning her own arms to her sides in a move she'd learned to break before puberty. Without thought, moving through motions she could carry out in her sleep, Zasha rammed her head back hard, attempting to slam the back of her skull into her attacker's face, hopefully breaking his nose.

But he possessed some skill in defense, yanking

his face back just in time ... and also momentarily weakening his hold on her. She slammed her butt back into his pelvis to carve out distance between her and the man holding her, then whipped her arms up, bent at the elbows, breaking his hold.

Several more men rushed to attempt to grab her from all sides, but now this was a situation she was ready for. Four tall, apparently strong men against one small woman? When that woman was her, she'd take those odds all day long.

Allowing the depth of her grief to fuel her rage, she spun and struck out like a viper, jabbing one in the throat and another in the eyeballs. The first gasped violently, struggling to draw breath. The other wailed an inhuman keen, clutching at his eyes.

Hands up in loose, open fists so she could punch or strike, Zasha protected her face and chest, spinning while bouncing on her feet to determine the next best point of attack.

She feinted to the left, then lunged right, snapping a coiled kick and taking out another man's knee. He crumbled to the ground with an agonized cry while she spun to take out the last man before Throat and Eyes could recover enough to come at her again. Knee wasn't getting back up.

Zasha circled the final man and decided she could take him down in a head-on fight—a few sharp jabs and kicks in the right places, a bone twisted beyond its breaking point, and she'd be free.

She danced across dark oily asphalt, skimming its surface, snapped her fist out to punch him in the nose, struck him in the side of the neck on the carotid artery, before latching on to the fingers he extended toward her and breaking several of them.

A moment before her fist smashed into the man's nose, a realization slammed into her.

Why his fingers were extended.

That he was mumbling words under his breath she didn't register.

What both those factors must mean.

And then she felt his attack.

Mere moments from her victory, he hit her with the one thing she wasn't prepared to defend against, no matter how many thousands of hours she'd spent in her family's gym.

Magic.

Without any real exposure to it before, she still knew exactly what it was.

And she understood that whatever magic this was, it was dark. The darkest.

Either that, or all magic was horrible.

A light so dark that it was basically shadow struck her square in the chest.

And despite all the strength and resilience Zasha had, she didn't have magic.

Rumors of magic swept across the underworld of Flaming Arrow. It was difficult to entirely avoid the stories of witches and wizards who could defy the laws of nature, or of the monsters who shouldn't exist. Those in her inner circle—her dad, her uncles, their families, the boys and a few girls who came to learn to fight—they had bigger things to worry about, like survival. Flaming Arrow would eat you alive and spit out your bones if you let it.

She stared blankly up at her assailant when the pulse of power knocked the breath out of her. Gasping, she struggled to suck in air, clutching uselessly at her throat.

But her sudden inability to fill her lungs wasn't her most pressing problem.

The darkness that clung to this magic was trying to consume her.

She understood the path this cloying darkness intended to take as if it spoke to her, as if it were becoming one with her—when she'd never wanted anything to do with the darkness that slunk along the secret alleyways and corners of Flaming Arrow. When she'd fought against it without identifying it her entire life.

She had to halt the flow of this magic. She *had* to keep it from consuming her.

Only ... she didn't know how to stop it.

Her mouth hung open, desperation urging her to continue sucking in breath. Yet the air she pulled in didn't make it past her throat. Tears stung the back of her eyeballs; she refused to let them fall. If she couldn't stop these men from killing her, so be it. But she would *not* let them break her before she died.

Her father and uncles didn't allow anyone possessed of magic to spar or fight in their gym. Magic users had an unfair advantage, and even if they swore not to use their powers, people with magic never played fair. Everyone in Flaming Arrow knew that.

She'd mastered a few hundred ways to kill the four men with her bare hands. After what they'd done, she would have enjoyed every single one of them.

And yet she was defenseless against the true firepower of their attack.

Eyes stinging, she sucked in air like she never had before, but was rewarded only with emptiness. With the promise of death. Her vision blurred and clouded around the edges.

She'd prepared her entire life to defeat entitled assholes like these, only to have her training fail her.

It was a crushing realization ... and Zasha was already broken. Devastated.

Wondering fleetingly if she'd see her papa or if there'd be nothing after this, she tried to pull in another breath and failed. Her knees weakened and brought her to the ground. Abstractly, she sensed the asphalt cold and damp beneath her jeans. They'd be soaked with filth and urine and whatever other foulness contributed to the unique scent of this part of town—an acrid bitterness like burnt tires and unwashed bodies that coated the air—the one she would have avoided at this time of night if not for her father.

Her eyelids closed of their own accord, shutting out the blurry images of the four men crowded around her.

Crumbling further so that she slumped over her knees, *At least I won't have to mourn Papa*, she thought. Though the fact that she should die the same day he did when so many of his decisions centered around giving her the best life possible only served to piss her the hell off.

She fought for air one last time...

And managed to suck in a ragged, wheezing breath that barely filled her lungs.

But it wasn't empty!

Greedily, ready to give the fight for her survival

every single bit of herself, she breathed in deeply, filling her lungs—

She froze.

Darkness swirled through her, traveling along the path of her breath, taking its time, as if it already possessed her entirely.

Trashing and clawing at her clothes, Zasha resisted what couldn't be prevented. Never before had she felt her soul, but in that moment she imagined she could feel it revolting inside her, refusing the darkness that sought to claim it.

Once more, useless.

In a swift moment, faster than she could accept what was happening, the dark magic overpowered her soul.

Her soul.

Despite its innate brightness, her soul—or whatever burned within her like a constant flame—wasn't able to defend itself.

Shadow wormed its way through every pulsing part of her body, taking over, consuming her like a plague. Suddenly, her survival became as alarming as what she'd believed was her impending end.

It didn't feel like this was their way to kill her.

Those same arms that had encircled her before latched on to her again, dragging her upward.

This time, she couldn't fight. Large monolithic

slabs of dark gunk weighed down her spirit, clamping down on her will to resist.

"Shit. She's a girl," one of the men commented as he peered into the shadows beneath her oversized hood.

Another of the men knocked the hood back off her head. He grunted in distaste. "Not a girl, a woman."

"A young woman, then," the first said as if annoyed to be corrected.

"Girl or woman, this isn't good. What do we do?" the third asked while the grip that clamped her from behind tightened. She was able to move, but in a foggy, intoxicated way, like she wasn't in true control of her body.

Blinking hazily, she continued to focus on listening. Even though their voices were garbled as they filtered through to her, she needed to learn what was happening to her.

"Do we let her go?" the first one, with his distinctive nasally voice, asked. "Boss doesn't want ladies in the Pound, not unless they're ones he asked for."

"That's no lady," said the one with magic, the only one Zasha feared.

She blinked groggily, trying to study him.

In a Henley shirt, its sleeves artfully pushed up above his elbows; dark skinny jeans, which looked too tight and uncomfortable to properly fight in; and flat boots, their leather shining in the dim light of a sliver of moon, he looked like the kind of person she would have discounted as posing no threat to her.

"Look at her," the magic man continued. "She's got no class, no finesse. She's dressed like a teenager who lives out on the streets. Her jeans and sneakers have holes in them, and her hoodie is huge, like she's some ganger. She looked like a boy from behind, and your boss likes the young boys with enough spark in them to fight back but not to win. You know that. Your boss won't care that she's a woman. She has enough fight in her for him to like her."

"He's your boss too," said the first man, who'd since delegated her restraint to the third man, since it was obvious now that she wouldn't resist.

"No." The man with magic propped his hands on his hips and stared at her. "He's not my boss, he just thinks he is. Big difference."

The three other men hmphed and grunted.

"We need one more, so we bring her," Magic Man said. "It's late, I want to get home, and I'm not in the mood to deal with your boss' tantrums. Unless one of you wants to tell him we're one short?" He looked at the other three, who didn't say anything, one shaking his head. "Her tits won't matter anyway. She'll be dead within a week, just like all the rest of them. More like, she'll be dead by tomorrow. She won't make it out of the ring."

A spark of something akin to hope flared within her. The ring was the one place where she knew exactly what to do to survive.

So long as the odds were fair and no one used magic...

Her eyes shut again without her direction while the men dragged her from the dark, forgotten corner of Flaming Arrow to another world entirely.

CHAPTER TWO

ZASHA

A DEEP, damp, and penetrating cold woke her long before she'd rested enough to recover from whatever the magic had done to her. Zasha opened her eyes slowly, certain she wouldn't like what she saw.

Her surroundings weren't all that different from what they'd been when she'd last been awake. She lay huddled on a hard, dank, and stained concrete floor.

Groaning, she tried to control the trembling in her body before her teeth started chattering. Wherever she was, she wasn't planning on staying, and the sooner she understood her circumstances, the sooner she could map out her escape.

Pushing herself to sitting, she managed only to lean on her hands but not to sit upright. *Weak.* She felt weak in a way she'd never felt before. And it wasn't just the thought of a world without her father in it. This was all-consuming, and she didn't like it. Not at all.

Gritting her teeth together, she swallowed a grunt as she forced herself to sit, scooting across the disgusting floor to lean against a concrete wall, which was freezing, and she was grateful to discover herself still wrapped in the thick hoodie. Flaming Arrow wasn't a safe place for women out on their own; it was only her signature knee-to-balls move that had saved her from becoming just one more victim of rape. Most of the girls who ended up in her dad's gym came to learn how to defend themselves from rapists, and most of them, though young, had learned of the prevalence of rape the worst way.

With difficulty, Zasha stretched her legs out in front of her, but she did it. Breathing slowly to remain calm, she counted that one blessing. At least she could now breathe freely.

Absently, she rubbed at her chest, thinking of her papa, and how many times she'd seen him do the same thing. She dropped her hand, worrying at the ache deep inside her, before shoving that concern away.

She heard her Uncle Andrei's familiar voice

echoing through her memories: *Focus on what you can do, not what you can't. Focusing on perceived weaknesses only undermines your strength.* Uncle Andrei said it in the deep, thick accent that neither her father nor her uncles had ever been able to kick.

Zasha chuffed to herself. "Look at where all their sacrifices got me," she whispered to the cold, cavernous cell.

She was definitely in a cell. The lack of windows anywhere in the walls, and the very small one set high in the closed door, with a small metal hatch that must slide open and closed from the other side, gave it away. Still, the second Zasha could stand up, she was trying that exit. Only the stupid and complacent operated on assumptions. She was neither. Just as soon as she could, she was going to test every lock and seam to see if she could break them.

Arching her neck, she examined the ceiling, wondering what exactly the asshole with magic had done to her to make that slight movement a chore.

The ceiling was plain cement as well, several droplets of moisture hanging heavily, preparing to drop, though none directly above her. There was nothing to hang on to anywhere to gain momentum for any sort of attack against the structural integrity of the cell.

"Damn," she muttered softly, not much more than an exhale. If her kidnappers didn't realize she was awake, she wasn't about to draw their attention to her.

At least the feeling that darkness was sweeping through her, claiming her, was gone. As she controlled her breathing and convinced her mind that cold was just an illusion, she began to roll her wrists and ankles. It might take longer than it should, but she needed her body limber if she was going to achieve anything resembling an escape.

Whenever someone came to check on her, she had to be ready. She wouldn't allow a single opportunity to pass her by without taking advantage of it.

Life favors the prepared.

Well, life had mostly screwed her over, but things would have been so much worse if she hadn't trained to gain every advantage she could. Flaming Arrow probably would have devoured her and licked its greedy chops long ago if she hadn't transformed herself into the kind of person who didn't go down easily.

Only she had gone down all too easily.

All it had taken was magic, the one thing she wasn't prepared for, and couldn't be. Magic didn't run in her blood.

The thought left a bitter taste in her mouth,

which already tasted like she'd partied all night, puked, and was waking with all the regret—and sourness—of the night's previous proclivities.

Gradually, sensation returned to her fingers and toes, unleashing a tidal wave of tingles that made her grit her teeth against the uncomfortable sensation. But now that she was becoming more alert, she was mindful of the sounds she made, and she wouldn't release another peep.

In this cell, she had few advantages. The element of surprise might be the only one available to her, and she was going to maximize it as much as she could.

Slowly, and with discomfort that bordered on pain, she forced herself into a crouch. Her calves and thighs came awake with agonizing intensity, but in order to fight, she had to be limber, and she currently felt like a big, heavy log.

It wouldn't do.

As her thoughts became crisper, while she moved she focused on listening, hoping to pick up sounds that would give her information she could use in her defense. Feeling as if she'd been KO'd the night before in a fight by a big, ugly, muscled brute, she made herself move through her usual warm-up.

When she lost a fight, and her opponent punished her hard, the next day everything hurt.

This is no different, she told herself, even though it most certainly was.

But *a fight is won in the mind before it's won in the ring*. That she knew without a doubt to be true.

Still crouched, she moved into one bent thigh and then the other, shifting her body weight back and forth, forcing her limbs to awaken, to ready.

After far too long, she managed to banish the cold and make her way to standing. At first, she wavered, and flung a hand out against a wall to catch herself.

But she managed to remain upright, and kept moving through her usual warm-up until her movements picked up speed, and she began to feel a bit like her usual self. She swung her arms in circles, the joints complaining less; she kicked and punched into the cold air, ignoring the way her breath clouded in front of her. As she built her own heat, her kicks and strikes were slow, but she was no quitter, her actions gradually becoming elegant once more—smooth and strong, like a caged cat that knew its moment will come.

The familiarity of her workout eased the panic that had tried to bloom inside her. This, she could do. This was what she knew. The pit of despair, which darkness had filled to the brim when the men had taken her, was moving to the background, where she'd make sure she forgot it.

Even thoughts of her papa barely managed to infiltrate the iron will she was enveloping herself in. She pushed away his death, what his absence would feel like as she continued to live, and she shoved away thoughts of her uncles too. Surely by now they'd noticed her missing and they'd sounded the alarm. Their wives and children, who were nearly as tough as they were, would be out looking for her. As would the gym regulars.

In Flaming Arrow, people took care of their own. Her uncles wouldn't call the police; they'd hit the streets, muscle-bound and furious, until they found her.

Only, would they?

She'd had a flip phone on her when the men had taken her. Ordinarily, she had no use for cell phones and most technology other than the beat-up TV she and her papa watched when they needed to veg after a particularly hard workout. With her dad going into the hospital though, she'd known she'd need to call someone.

But the flip phone was gone. She didn't need to pat the front kangaroo pocket of her hoodie to know. The damn thing always bounced around in there when she moved, which was one of the reasons she couldn't stand to carry it around.

Rolling her neck, she was pleased to discover she was warming up quite nicely. Sure, she didn't feel as limber and confident as usual, but she'd get there.

She had to.

Sounds.

She rushed to the door and pressed an ear to the cold metal. A clank, as if a door like hers had been slammed shut.

Then nothing.

Rising onto her tiptoes, she peeked through the small window at the top of the door. It was maybe five by seven inches; threads of steel wove through the glass. Not that breaking it would do her much good. It was too high up to allow her to squeeze an arm through and reach the handle below. And there was nothing in the cell with her that would serve as a tool. Even so, ideas of smashing the window and using her hoodie to hook the handle raced through her mind. It wasn't a plan likely to lead to success, but she'd consider all avenues that might get her out of here.

When she didn't see anything but a blank hallway as bleak as her cell, she pressed a cheek against the glass, turning this way and that, hoping to make out something that would help.

Nothing beyond a bare bulb up the hall from her; she couldn't even tell how long the hallway was, or how many cells like hers there might be.

Which led her to wonder once more: Why had they taken her? What did they want with her? If anyone tried to rape her or pass her around like some plaything for men who possessed too much power and too little sense of decency, she'd make them regret it; she had no doubt. If she went out, she'd go out in a blaze of mutilated penises and testicles that would ensure the "men" would never inflict their depravity on anyone else.

They'd regret having taken her. She'd make sure of it.

Another clank of a door, and her heartbeat sped up.

Two doors. Did that mean there were two others trapped in here like her? It could mean that, or the sound of doors opening and closing could be of just one cell, or of another room that didn't house a person.

The murmur of voices, too soft to make out, along with the shuffle of footsteps.

She stilled.

Should she attack now? Was this her one chance to get out of here? Or should she pretend to still be sleeping and bide her time while she gathered information that would help the chances of success of her breakout?

She bit the insides of her lip while she debated, thankful her mind was working as usual, cycling through pros and cons rapidly.

She cursed under her breath. It was a crapshoot. Without more awareness of her circumstances, she couldn't make a sound decision. But once she had that information, the element of surprise might be gone.

The decision was stolen from her.

Fire raced through her veins, vanishing any thoughts of the cold that had previously afflicted her. The flames incinerated every part of her insides, forcing her to her knees. She fell too hard, and the bone of her kneecaps slammed against the concrete, sending agony whipping through her.

The fire overshadowed it, making any discomfort unimportant as she suddenly found herself gasping for breath, much as she had when the men took her.

Only this time, no magic kept her from sucking in those precious inhales.

The fire—the devastating and all-consuming flame—made it impossible to do anything but struggle to survive, to endure, to make it to the other side of whatever this was.

She gasped, pulling in ragged breaths, while a

fleeting question managed to filter through the flames: Would her mind melt? Was this magic again? It had to be. Was the magic setting fire to her ability to think, and would she be a useless vegetable afterward?

A scream rang through the room, bouncing off the walls, floor, and ceiling long before she realized it was hers. Once she did, she couldn't prevent the next one from following the first.

Agony and desperation ripped through her, hooking into her and tearing her apart, as she begged to gods she didn't believe in for the torment to end.

She'd endured suffering. Hell, her whole life had been about taking the hit and getting back up. But this was the kind of strike no one would ever get back up from again. This ... wasn't right. Her insides contorted in ways she couldn't identify. All she knew was hurt. Every bit of her uniqueness, every part of her that defined the woman she was, was swallowed up in one big gulp, gone to her forever she feared.

She slammed back into the hard floor, writhing against the sensations that weren't hers, that weren't human, that no one should ever have to feel. Her head snapped back, hitting the concrete, and she screamed out her humanity. Gone was the grief for the loss of her father, the one man who'd made her feel safe in an ugly world. Gone was the anger at her mother, who'd made life difficult for a man who deserved good things more than anyone else she'd ever known. Gone were fleeting wishes that her uncles and her little tribe would come rushing in to save her. Once her mother left, she'd tried never to rely on anyone to help her; she'd mostly saved herself. But now she'd take being a damsel in distress. She'd do anything to make it end.

She even welcomed death. Anything had to be better than this.

Against her will, her hands and toes curled in on themselves, fighting what she didn't know how to resist. Her back arched, sliding her along the grimy floor.

She tried to bring her knees up toward her chest, but she only did for a few quick moments before they flung out in front of her, her entire body going rigid for a few scant moments. Like an orgasm, her body clenched against the overwhelming sensations rushing through her. Unlike an orgasm, she pleaded for it to finish, swallowing her whimpers as she sucked in useless breaths.

Then, respite arrived.

Every muscle loosened, and she melted like putty onto the floor, never more grateful to be lying in filth.

She had only time for hope to glimmer inside her

before the pain returned with as much ferocity as the arc of a sword, swinging to slice off her head.

She wished for a swift death, and then a force as violent as any white-water-rapids swept away every remaining wish and thought.

She would have hung on, trying to keep her sanity, a sense of herself, but it was pointless. She knew it. She let go of everything that made her who she was and fell into the pain. It tore through her as angrily as a rabid beast, bent on maximum destruction. A wail echoed off the walls as she clenched her eyes shut, bit her tongue, and swallowed blood, her invisible enemy slicing, bludgeoning, and ripping through her insides, tearing every organ and piece of flesh apart. The miraculous design of the human body was overcome by the same darkness as before. Hazily, she recognized it, and understood its intent.

To destroy. To change. To transform.

To shift.

But to shift into what?

From somewhere beyond her, she thought she heard someone else scream. Maybe several someones. Or it could have all been her.

She couldn't tell. She couldn't think.

She no longer knew if she could survive this.

No longer knew if she wanted to.

Then every muscle tensed once more, and the ripping, shredding, and rending resumed.

Whoever would emerge after this would no longer be her. There was no chance of it. Sanity couldn't survive torture like this.

Humans couldn't survive this.

CHAPTER THREE

ZASHA

SOMEWHERE ALONG THE unrelenting path of her torment, a new darkness crept in that was unlike the one seizing control of her body. She recognized it for what it was. Relief. An escape from the fracturing of her physical form. Possibly even of her mind.

In the ring, there'd been many occasions when the blackout had claimed her. But every fighter resisted it. To be knocked out was to be thoroughly defeated. And so she'd learned to recognize the signs and evade capture.

This time, she ran toward unconsciousness as a child ran toward the ocean, seeing it for the first time. She prayed to some unknown entity to take her away from the pain. To sweep her from this life, and the unknown entity she prayed to with a desperate, breaking mind didn't respond, but the blackness rushed in regardless, dimming her sight, deepening her breathing from the shallow agonized gasps to the steady rhythm of sleep in a place where the ordinary couldn't reach.

She had no idea if she slept, or how long she did so. All she knew was an absence of that pain, and she would have given an entire additional lifetime with her papa just to escape that agony—so long as he led the healthy life and she was the one missing out.

She was almost glad her father wouldn't be around to see what was happening to her. It would break him in a way that his wife leaving him had never managed.

She had always been his *volchok*—his precious, little wolf. He'd dreamt of grandeur for her beyond the borders of Flaming Arrow when she'd been unwilling to.

To see what was becoming of her ... after all the sacrifices he made to give her the best life he could ... well, it would kill him all over again.

And a man's heart could break but once.

Hers, well, her physical heart, the organ that still somehow beat inside her, must be a big, pulpy mass of mush. Nothing could survive what she'd just endured. She wasn't the same. Even without the energy to examine herself, she knew so. She *felt* how different she was. The dark magic she'd avoided all her life simmered inside her like a disease with no cure.

She'd never thought of herself as a particularly good person. Never one that anyone would really look up to beyond the misguided kids from the gym. But she also hadn't thought of herself as a bad person. She never stole or did anything she realized would hurt another. She cursed like any of the guys who frequented the gym and fought hard enough to gain their grudging respect. She bitched about the unfairness of life when it got her down, but she didn't let it keep her down for long. She was a good daughter and a good niece, and a good cousin to her uncles' children.

She was solidly middle-of-the-road okay.

But now ... now, she felt an ugly wickedness circulating through her veins, and she understood then it wouldn't be possible to be the same Zasha Volkov ever again. Something fundamental about her had shifted forever. The dark magic within clung to her, continuing to morph who she was.

Finally, she opened her eyes. As if they were crusty blinds that hadn't been used in decades, even that movement required far too much effort.

She was lying facedown on the floor of the cell, arms and legs curled beneath her. From her vantage point, she could make out gouges in the grime surrounding her, reaching deep into the cement. If that had been her, she must have torn up all her fingernails. The gouges were finger-distance apart.

Scents, suddenly so much stronger, assaulted her nose, awakening it fully. She smelled not only her own fear and pain, but also feces, vomit, and urine. Some of the urine was her own, most somebody else's —several somebody elses.

Stunned, she realized there was more buried within the scents. She could tell there were at least a dozen other people nearby, or at least that many people had recently come and gone, which was possible. Who would want to stay here if they had a choice?

Her mind foggy and slow to process—as was usual after a hard knockout, and this had been the hardest of her life—she worked to force herself to process the signs around her. Perhaps her captors would underestimate her, thinking her still incapacitated from the pain, and she'd manage her escape after all.

If she did, she was gathering her uncles Andrei, Vadim, Iosif, Yegor, and Lev, their families, every ally she had from the gym, and she was hunting down the assholes who'd taken her. Her "family" would rally to her side. There wasn't much her father and uncles had preserved from their motherland, insisting that since they were in America, they should act like it. But they had imported their sense of vengeance. They'd never wanted to let it go. They said that was how their people ruled themselves, a derivative of the law of might. If a crime went unpunished, the miscreant would see no reason not to do it again. But break a finger or two, and that person would never do what they'd done again. Her Uncle Yegor liked to say this was efficient. Better to break someone's fingers now, he'd say, then have to cut off their whole hand later.

There was a poetic justice in that, she'd always thought. At least with them you knew where you stood, and wherever you were in their esteem, you were the one who put yourself there. Whereas when magic was involved, the rules of the playground jumped out the window.

Busy fantasizing about how her family would join in destroying the people who'd done this to her, she startled when she picked up the sounds of footfalls and voices drawing near.

Two men. No, three. One was walking on one leg and a crutch of some sort. They all weighed around one-eighty to two-hundred pounds. One lighter on his feet than the other two.

One of the men's breathing was labored, the

other grunted while he walked. The one with the crutch, she thought.

As they drew closer and she realized they were likely coming to her cell, she recognized their scents and froze, a low, deep growl rumbling through her.

These were three of the four men who'd attacked her. The one breathing oddly was the one she'd struck in the throat. She suspected she'd fractured cartilage in his larynx. The second one, walking with a crutch, was the one whose knee she kicked; she'd almost certainly broken something.

And the third…

The growling deepened in her belly.

The third was the one who'd infected her with this dark magic.

He was the one responsible for her being here.

Which meant that he was the one she needed to kill first.

Revenge, yes. Punishment. But also he needed to learn not to take people from the streets. From anywhere.

She would make sure he could never take anyone else. Somehow…

As a key rasped inside the lock to her door, she stood, noticing for the first time how much was wrong—other than the obvious point of her captivity.

But she couldn't focus on that just yet. She was

too busy noticing how thick the door was, and how the lock didn't extend all the way through the door. The bolt could only be accessed from the front, and the door was thick enough to allow this—maybe three or four inches.

That was odd. If they were in the business of sequestering those they figured too weak to resist, why did they need doors this thick? It didn't add up.

Her hackles rose as the man with magic stepped into the room first, immediately wrinkling his nose. He yanked his face back while his lips pinched in evident disgust.

She snarled and fantasized about kicking his legs out from under him, straddling him, and snapping his neck. It would be over in seconds.

She smiled. The man with magic caught the gesture and stumbled backward a step before realizing what he'd done. Nervously, she thought, he regained the lost ground.

"What's taking you guys so long?" he barked out the door, and Throat and Knee stepped in. Or rather, gimped in.

A line the width of the side of her hand blemished Throat's neck. And Knee, well ... Knee might never walk properly again, which would serve him right for what he did.

As Knee moved to flank Magic Man, stopping a

step behind him, he shot her a look that was equal parts rage and fear. His eyeballs vibrated with the emotions, visibly quivering, and she scented the fear on him more strongly than the anger.

Good. He should be scared of her. She wouldn't be broken forever. Whatever they'd done to her, it was bound to wear off sometime, and then they'd really learn what it was to be sorry.

Throat sniffed loudly, drawing her attention, and she realized he was actually sucking up mucus. A moment before he hawked a loogie at her, she coiled her legs and bounded out of the way.

The slimy lump of phlegm and mucus splattered on the floor, an inch from where she'd only just been, quivering like pudding.

She sneered at him. Disgusting.

But as she registered the oddity of her movements, she smelled a shift in their scents. Surprise. Appreciation.

And she knew there was no way that was good.

They'd left the door open behind them, but the faint thread of light that streamed in wouldn't have been necessary for her examination of herself anyway. Her eyesight was incredible. She'd never needed glasses, and so she was used to seeing everything well. But this was a whole new level of seeing. Even in the dimness, she could make out the grittiness of the concrete, where the droplets of moisture above eventually fell and marred the floor with grooves. The slight crack along the juncture of two walls in her cell. The way the hinges to the door were reinforced, anticipating that someone far stronger than her would attempt to break out.

What did they keep in here? Even as strong as she was, she wasn't that strong. Nobody was.

Worse though—so much worse—she'd anticipated what she might see even before she looked down. She could smell herself. And she'd never smelled like fur before. She shouldn't smell like fur.

The man with magic was about to talk, she could tell. How, she wasn't sure; probably the way he breathed in and his jaw creaked softly as he opened it, loud to her ears.

But she was busy looking down at her feet and facing a reality too outrageous to process easily.

She'd known there was something wrong with her gait, with her movements, with how low to the ground she moved—the way she stood on four feet instead of two, once she stopped to process, and how those feet weren't really feet but paws with thick, dense pads on the bottom of them.

"Oh, look," Knee said. "She's only just now figuring out she's a wolf." He guffawed along with

Throat, until she snapped her head up and snarled at them.

Fear wafted off Knee and he demonstrated more intelligence than she thought him capable of by shutting the hell up before she snapped his leg off entirely and rammed it down his throat.

She suspected the nature of her thoughts was evident on her face—whatever it looked like. Knee half hopped, half walked, retreating out the door.

Magic Man huffed, but didn't take his eyes off her as if he seemed to realize the danger she posed. And she was more dangerous then than she'd ever been in her entire life.

The dark magic still swam inside her, threatening to drown her, but she'd survive long enough to take the assholes with her to whatever hell accepted furry, monstrous things like her.

She'd registered it before looking up: thick, rich fur covering legs that were undoubtedly animal legs and not her strong, limber, muscular legs—her *human* legs.

"Where the hell do you think you're going? Get your ass back here," Magic Man snapped at Knee.

"Un-unh," Knee said, wobbling on his crutch, his face paling.

She snarled at him, hoping he'd piss himself. He was close to losing control of his bladder, she could tell. The scent of fear wafted off him. Sour, foul, ripe.

"She looks unstable," he said. "And she was crazy to begin with. I'll take my chances with the boss."

Unstable? she thought. *Crazy?* What had he expected her to do when they attacked? Say *yes please* and *thank you*?

She'd already understood that they'd only attacked her because she was bent over, a wisp of her usual self, drowning in grief. But now she *really* understood.

They picked only on the weak and the vulnerable, the ones who couldn't fight back for whatever reason. They didn't expect a fight because they didn't usually get it.

Which made what they did all the worse.

They preyed on those who most needed their protection. The weaker links of society, the ones her papa and uncles always went out of their way to look out for.

Her family's gym, named Gold Gym, was as much a space of training as an informal community center. If someone was down on their luck, neither her father nor his brothers would turn them away. Her family wasn't running a charity—couldn't afford to—so they'd put the strays to work to earn their keep. But they'd give them a place and a sense of value.

Show them they were needed. That they could contribute.

An odd sensation swept across her until she realized it was her hackles rising even more. Men like these were the entire reason Flaming Arrow was such a dangerous place to live. Entire neighborhoods within the city were peaceful, just hoping men like these would leave them alone.

But there had always been men like these. And that's why there would always be places like Flaming Arrow, where good people like her father and uncles had to work so hard to make a life for themselves and their families.

Knee gone, Throat rubbed anxiously at his neck. "She does look like she wants to kill us," he said.

"They all look like that at the start," Magic Man said, but from the fear vibrating off Throat, it was clear that wasn't true.

Throat started to back up. Magic Man whipped a hand out to keep him there.

"She'll die like the rest of them soon enough. Nothing to worry about."

Only there definitely was something to worry about. She still didn't know what kind of monster she'd turned into exactly, only that she was no longer anything she recognized. That mattered, it most definitely did, but it didn't much matter right then.

She could eviscerate them first, and ask questions later.

Throat had called her a wolf, but she didn't know what being a wolf felt like. And she didn't trust him to speak the truth.

So slowly that she hoped they wouldn't realize, she approached them. They hadn't moved far beyond the door, and the cell was large, as if designed to hold many people—or monsters.

Within a few more paces, she was going to attack. She had no idea how this body worked yet or how far she could jump. All she knew was that she felt strong despite the darkness swirling inside her like an insidious fog.

She suspected she could pounce on both of them —Magic Man first—and take them both down before Throat could run away screaming.

But before she could attack, Throat apparently decided he feared her more than Magic Man.

He jerked his arm free of Magic Man's hold, spun on his heel, and ran.

Magic Man lost sight of her for a second while he turned to watch Throat go, yelling at him to stop.

She sprang from a crouch and slammed into his twisted torso, taking him down.

He landed with a hollow thud on the floor, arms flinging upward to protect his face.

They wouldn't do him enough good.

Her maws stretched open and she snapped them down on his face, puncturing cheek, snagging his lower lip, and scraping across teeth and chin.

She froze.

Blood slipped into her mouth, but she couldn't move, not even to spit it out.

"Get off him," a taller, older man said in a gravelly voice.

He spoke some words in a rush that she didn't identify. Then, from her peripheral vision, she saw him fling his hands in her direction. A millisecond before his spell hit, she understood what was coming.

A flash and then something that felt like rope lassoed her body, pulling the cords of the spell tightly around her, yanking.

Since her teeth hadn't moved, she took a chunk of Magic Man's cheek with her.

Then she was flying toward the wall.

A rigid mass unable to roll or otherwise prepare herself for the impact, she hit hard, and slid like a rock down to the floor.

"Stay," the tall man said.

She had no choice but to obey.

Once more, a man with magic had commandeered her free will.

Magic.

The one thing she didn't have and didn't know how to fight.

She thumped to the floor and toppled over onto her side and waited for this other man to declare her fate.

If he let her go, she'd kill him first, and Magic Man second.

Guaranteed.

CHAPTER FOUR

ZASHA

IN HER MIND, which turned out not to be a melted mess as she'd feared, Zasha thrashed and bucked and snarled.

And yet ... in the dark, dank space of her cell, the only sounds were those of Magic Man, who cried with pain, and that of the tall man, who breathed deeply and calmly as he bent over at the waist, studying her.

"Having trouble breathing, are we?" he asked.

Whatever troubles she had, they all stemmed from him—assuming he was the boss.

So desperate was her desire to kill her captors and break free, she hadn't even realized her breathing was once more labored. But now that she paid attention, she saw that he was right.

A chunk of Magic Man's cheek sat in her mouth,

leaning against her tongue and teeth as her face rested on its side.

She wanted to spit out the flesh, preferably hit one of the two men in the face with it, but even her breath came as if she were sipping through a straw. She was sure that modest bit of air she managed to pull in was only due to Boss' desire to keep her alive.

For his purposes, no doubt.

He twisted his fingers in the space between her and him and the pathway to her lungs opened. However, she wouldn't give him the satisfaction of witnessing her relief. She held his stare evenly until he looked away—to continue studying the rest of her.

Desperate to snarl, growl, and bite, she still could do none of those things.

"Quite an incredible specimen," Boss said, but not to her. "For a bitch, her size and musculature is impressive."

I'll show you who's a bitch, she thought, shooting death daggers at him with her eyes.

"I was upset at first when I heard you'd brought me a bitch when you know I have no use for bitches," he continued, ignoring the muffled cries of Magic Man, the one who'd claimed Boss didn't give him orders. Clearly, he'd been blowing hot air. Pain glazed Magic Man's eyes, and yet he tried not to make a sound, swallowing much of his anguish.

"But this one is remarkable." Boss studied her as if he believed she was his property. "She's as big as the males."

He chuckled, as if oblivious to the pain of everyone else in the room with him. Worse, she suspected he didn't mind it.

"Granted," he said, "the boys you bring me are weak and smaller than they should be for the most part. I don't think she'll come close to matching the size of a true alpha, or even one of their betas."

He shook his head and smiled in a way that chilled her blood. That gesture confirmed what she was starting to suspect. Not only did this man not flinch at the discomfort of others, he enjoyed it.

What kind of man relished the pain of other living beings?

"A true werewolf or wolf shifter would tear her to pieces," he added, his smile widening. "Wouldn't that be a sight to see..." He tilted his head to one side. "A shame it will never happen."

With a slight belly that curved over crisp jeans, he stood, placing a hand in one of his back pockets. A dark blue turtleneck wrapped his neck, and he flicked an unconcerned hand through artfully messy hair of an indeterminate brown. A few strands of gray tinted the hair above his ears.

He tipped his head the other way as he studied

her. "Even so, I'll schedule the biggest fight for her. Her eyes are angry."

You got that right, asshole, she thought.

He moved his hand from his hair to his chin, considering. "Who of the wolves is sufficiently recovered to fight her?" he asked Magic Man, unconcerned that the wizard clearly was in no position to speak.

As Zasha once more attempted to swallow her saliva—and probably some of Magic Man's face too—she wondered how much damage she might have inflicted on him. Enough to threaten his life if no one staunched the bleeding? Unlikely, but she could still hope.

She was unable to swallow while Boss still had a hold on her. She wasn't sure whether or not the magic ropes still bound her as her eyes weren't positioned at an angle to confirm that, but either way, she couldn't move.

Boss tsked in irritation. "You make me wait for an answer?"

"Um."

Zasha's attention shot to Throat, who apparently wasn't as intelligent as she'd credited him; when he ran, he hadn't gone far.

He leaned against the doorjamb, glanced at Magic Man, grimaced with empathy, and said, "Wild

Killer is sufficiently recovered, Boss. He'll be ready to fight in a few days."

"A few days?" Boss asked in a tone that sounded unconcerned, but made Throat wince.

"A couple of days at most," Throat squeaked, before clearing his throat a few times. Clearly, Zasha's strike had caused lasting damage by the way he followed that up with a visible struggle to swallow.

"Maybe," Throat labored on, even though Boss hadn't said anything else. "Maybe Wild Killer can be gotten ready in a day."

"Whoever does that will earn my favor," Boss said as if he were some magnanimous emperor instead of a prick who preyed on the defenseless.

"Yes, Boss. I'll get right on it," Throat said, earning a stare from Magic Man that could have been displeasure, but maybe not; it was hard to tell with how his face was contorted with grimaces beneath all the gaping skin and blood.

Did Magic Man fear Boss so much that he wouldn't even leave to tend his wound? The answer was obvious. Despite his earlier bravado, it was clear who ruled this roost.

"Have Wild Killer ready by tomorrow night," Boss said. "I'll start spreading the word. No one will want to miss out on this fight. She has just enough spunk in her to give him a run for his money. And then the kill will be all that much more spectacular." His eyes grew dreamy, as if Boss were fantasizing about watching Wild Killer murder Zasha.

She didn't think he did it to instill fear in her. No, she was pretty sure he didn't care what she felt one way or another. Boss was the kind of man who thought only about himself and his own pleasure. Which meant that he had to die. The world needed fewer men like this one. Like none.

Boss' words didn't frighten her. They motivated her.

Whoever this Wild Killer was, it sounded like she was going to get a chance in the ring with him. Sure, she was in a new form and there was this dark magic swirling around inside her that was in no way right. But at least in the ring, where Boss and Magic Man wouldn't hover above her with their spelled fingers at the ready, she had a chance of survival. Of freedom. To get out of here and then return to light the place up in a blaze of purification.

One chance was better than none.

Now what she needed was information. What would this ring be like? What were the rules of the fight?

Though from what she'd seen of the men, she could guess there probably wouldn't be any rules. No holds barred, and death of one's opponent secured victory.

She also needed to know about Wild Killer. His name suggested that he was both savage and vicious, but would she be fighting him in this ... wolf form? By now, she suspected that's what she'd become ... though she didn't understand. How could magic transform a person's nature? It didn't seem as if it should be able to do that.

She'd heard the term *werewolf* before of course, but only in stories that warned against the monsters. She'd never heard of a *wolf shifter*. Weren't they the same creature?

Her father and uncles didn't like to speak of such things, and did their best to change the subject whenever anyone brought up magic, treating it as if it were a foul word and an even fouler practice.

If Magic Man's dark magic had indeed transformed her into a wolf, did that make her a werewolf? Or a wolf shifter? Did that mean she would be able to change back into a human? And would she have to endure that much pain again when she did? As tough as she liked to think she was, she didn't know if she was courageous enough to willingly endure the agony that had eventually delivered her shift into this animal.

"What do you guess the bitch is thinking?" Boss

asked, seemingly to no one in particular. "She actually looks like she's ... considering her circumstances."

She heartily wished his hold over her would fail so she could bite off his face. His tone suggested surprise that she should be intelligent.

She visualized her teeth and claws free to attack him ... and felt a twinge of movement in all of those spots. She managed to swallow and push the chunk of Magic Man's cheek to the front of her mouth, where she'd spit it out at the earliest opportunity.

Too late, she realized that Boss followed her movements, and though they'd been slight, he noticed.

"Interesting," he said again, like she was some lab project and not a person. Her fantasies about how she'd kill him became more graphic in her mind, more violent.

And she twitched more.

Boss walked closer. "Most interesting."

That's it, she thought. *Come close enough for me to bite you.*

He halted in his approach, almost as if he'd heard her.

Could wizards read minds? She didn't know much about the world of magic other than to steer clear of it.

Boss straightened and rubbed his hands together

in front of him, a grin transforming his otherwise ordinary visage into something twisted and depraved.

"Oh, this is going to be so much fun. I have a feeling this fight is going to be one my patrons will speak of for years to come."

Then he turned and walked past Magic Man without a glance at him, and paused by Throat. "Get the wolf ready, and tell him we'll let him skip a fight if he draws this one out, making her beg for the kill."

Throat nodded, fear rolling off him, souring the already foul air. "Right. Gets a fight off. Got it."

"Of course," Boss continued pedantically, "he won't actually get a fight off. He makes me too much money. But motivation is good."

Throat just nodded, his limp hair flopping around on his head in his enthusiasm to please the man who towered over him by more than half a foot.

Then Boss finally looked at Magic Man. He frowned. "Get up, Marley. You need stitches."

He beckoned to Marley with a hand, not moving to help him up, though Marley was clearly overcome by the pain of his injury.

Zasha didn't particularly enjoy seeing suffering in anyone—generally. She was quite pleased, however, that she'd managed to inflict that much damage through one strike.

If only her uncles could have at them. In a fair

match, her uncles would mop the floor with their bodies. As a group, they were consistently muscled, strong, wicked fast, and fierce, exactly the kind of fighters she wanted on her side. Her dad had been as strong as any of them, until his heart started acting up too much. At the end, he trained others more than he trained himself, hoping no one would much notice the shift in his priorities.

Without waiting for Marley to stand, Boss swept out of the room.

The moment he was beyond her sight, she resumed her struggle against her bindings. But they didn't give any more.

So she watched Throat approach Marley with as much caution as if he were a wounded beast. Throat tentatively offered him a hand.

Marley narrowed his eyes at him, but seemed incapable of much more as he accepted the assistance. Leaning heavily into Throat, Marley, with blood dripping down his chin and neck, tread lightly as he turned to look at Zasha. If looks could kill, his would have left her doubly dead. A hand gripped his cheek gingerly; blood dripped from in between his fingers, sliding down his hand, soaking the sleeve of his sweater. Once a hunter green, the natural color of the yarn mixed with the blood and appeared a rusty brown.

"Come on, Marley," Throat said. "You can punish her later. Half your face looks like it's about to slide off. You need to be taken care of."

Zasha had an entirely different idea of what kind of taking care of Marley needed, and met his glare head on.

As the two men turned their backs to her, and shuffled toward the open door, she coiled her muscles in preparation. That much she could do now, but she could move no more than that.

When the men stepped beyond the doorway to her cell, she tensed all over, aching with the need to launch herself at their retreating forms—but mostly to escape through the open door.

But moments later, Throat pulled the door shut behind them with a final clank, and she heard Throat turning Marley, leaning the mage against him, while he locked the door and pocketed the key. With her wolf ears, she could make out the way the metal of the key—large, from the sounds—rustled against the fabric of his pants.

And then they shuffled away.

Zasha strained at the magical ropes that held her...

And broke free.

Already coiled and furious, she spit out the hunk of Marley's cheek and ran at the door, ramming into it with her front paws, rising onto her hind legs to push against it. The reinforced hinges creaked, but barely.

She'd missed her chance. The door was locked, offering no way out for her.

She wanted to unleash her anger and frustration against the door, on something tangible. She wanted to see results of her actions, even if they hurt her.

But she wouldn't.

She couldn't.

She had a fight to prepare for, and she was at too much of a disadvantage without tacking on poor choices.

Already, her ribcage ached from the impact of slamming into the wall. She needed to care for herself.

And ready herself.

She didn't know much about what she was or what she could do now. She didn't even know the time of day, or how long she had before "tomorrow night's" fight.

All she knew was that, despite the dark magic she sensed inside her like a living thing, she was still enough of the same Zasha she'd always been to get herself to do what needed to be done.

She would use her time wisely. She'd get to understand her wolf body as much as possible. She'd learn the ways she moved in this form, what she was capable of, and what limits her strength and agility had when she was on all fours.

She'd train and learn.

She'd prepare.

And she'd also rest and heal.

Her next fight would be the most important one in a long line of fights—of her life.

Too angry to rest yet, she began to move her new body through stretches and lunges, testing the extent of her reach, the range of her movements.

When the rage sufficiently abated, she lay on her belly, tucked her arms and legs beneath her, and closed her eyes to encourage her ribcage to heal.

Pushing away thoughts of how Boss' magic could reach her beyond the doorway to her cell, she encouraged herself into a healing sleep.

She could only afford a small slice of time. From here on out, she had to make the most of every minute she had. She was going to be putting to the test all the knowledge her dad and uncles ever gave her. They'd run from their motherland because they were hunted. Their techniques, the ones they imparted to her, originated from a visceral sense of survival.

She'd trained for this very moment—kind of—almost every single day since she was a girl.

If anyone could do this, she could.

Her breathing deepened, and she encouraged the healing that would accelerate with sleep.

She was a warrior.

And now she was a wolf.

Warriors didn't bitch and moan about uncertainties or unfairness, they sucked it up and got to business.

It's precisely what she would do. She could bitch and moan and grieve for the loss of her father and her humanity later.

For now, it was only about one thing.

Survival.

CHAPTER FIVE

ZASHA

ZASHA FOUND it difficult to calculate the passing of time in the darkness of her cell. All she knew was that there was far too little time for her to learn all the advantages at her disposal in her new form.

Regardless, it was going to have to do.

She'd spent all the time allotted to her alternating between testing her wolf body's limits and resting to ensure she was in top physical condition—within her current capability.

Someone had come to deliver food and water to her a couple of times, but she hadn't seen who. The person slid open the small piece of metal at the bottom of her door, all but tossed the food and water inside, sloshing half of it over the sides of the metal bowls, and then hastily shut the little door again, never once crossing a fingertip into her cell.

The person hadn't come to retrieve the empty containers either. A menstruating female, from the scent of her, she was fearful, cowed, and resigned.

Zasha didn't think the woman would attempt escape even if given the chance. Zasha suspected the men who ran this operation had broken her spirit.

No matter what they did to Zasha, that was one thing she would never allow. *Never*.

A low, vicious growl rumbled deep through her chest while she waited for someone to come fetch her for the fight. She knew it was time. She'd heard an increase in footfalls and voices. The energy tangibly ratcheted up a notch, thick with tension, anticipation, and satisfaction.

The satisfaction, of course, was not yet hers. Or of anyone beyond Boss, whose scent she picked up floating around in the space well beyond her door.

For half of the day, as she trained, she'd wondered whether there might be others like her trapped here. When they'd snatched her, Marley mentioned that they had to meet a quota of some sort, which implied that there were others held captive as she was.

Zasha paced back and forth in front of her door, wishing she knew how long it would be before they came to get her. Should she rest to preserve energy and endurance? Or should she remain warm and limber?

She doubted she'd be given time to stretch and warm up before they threw her in the ring.

Silence had settled for several minutes, but now footfalls slapped against a hard surface, probably the same dismal concrete as in her cell, and drew closer.

"You're going to have to muzzle her," the man with the nasally voice said, the one who'd helped capture her.

Another man grunted but didn't otherwise respond. Zasha thought it might be Marley. His scent grew stronger, but besides that she smelled antiseptic, dried blood, and pain.

"*I'm* not gonna muzzle her," Nasal said, leading Zasha to think Marley, though unwilling to speak because of his cheek and jaw, had indicated in some way that he was passing the buck to Nasal.

"Un-unh," Nasal said. "Barden told me all about what happened down here. I'm not going anywhere near her face."

Another grunt and, presumably, another gesture.

"Fine," Nasal spat. "But if you let her go, I'm going to hold you responsible for whatever happens."

Zasha's guess was that Marley wouldn't much care what happened to Nasal, and Nasal was right to sound so unsure. If Zasha got the chance, she was one-hundred percent ripping off his cheek too.

A key slid into the lock on the other side of her door, and Zasha positioned herself next to where the door would swing open, padding lightly on nimble paws.

The door unlocked, and a long pause drew out on the other side of the reinforced metal. Long enough for Zasha to wonder and worry at what the delay might mean.

The moment the door swung open, she understood.

Despite the fact that bandages, stained with a yellow of medicine, wrapped half of his face, Marley had managed to mutter a spell to hold at the ready, dark light arcing between his palms.

It was the same dark magic that had changed her forever, and she *hated* it. Hated him. She snarled in mid-motion, mid-leap. She'd been prepared, and the moment the door opened, she'd bounded at the men.

Wrapped in a cloud of light as dark as shadows, she hung suspended in mid-air.

She could no longer attack, but she could still tell him what she thought about that. She growled and snarled so ferociously that fear raced down the length of Nasal's body in a visible shudder.

Then her mouth froze, and flickers of dark light snapped in front of her vision, making her force her eyes shut in case they should burn her eyeballs. She had the sense Marley's magic could do that, and the way he was staring at her a bit too pleased with himself, while evil glints flicked in his shadowed eyes, she understood he was out for revenge and she shouldn't provoke him unnecessarily.

He probably only wasn't hurting her because he was more afraid of Boss than of her, no matter what he'd tried to claim earlier. If Marley feared a man more than a raging wolf, what was Boss Man capable of? What else did he do with his power and influence? The questions awakened old feelings deep in the pit of her stomach: righteous anger at injustice, desire to punish those who abused others.

Marley tossed his head at Nasal, who was busy staring at Zasha's wolf, wide-eyed. When Marley added a grunt to his unspoken command, Nasal scurried forward, fully entering the room, skirting along the wall so as not to touch the wolf.

"If you let her bite me," Nasal said, "I'll tell the boss you let her get me, and then you'll have to deal with him. You got me?"

Nasal had a short crew-cut and a hook nose. He alternated between shooting the wolf and Marley wary looks. Zasha kept her eyes closed, just in case, relying on her other augmented senses to understand what was going on.

Marley grunted something that sounded a lot like, "Won't care."

"The boss will too care. I've been loyal to him for four years. You've only been with him for seven months. If he has to pick, he'll pick me."

In response, Marley wagged the fingers of one hand.

Nasal pouted. "Magic isn't everything, you know."

But for Zasha right then, it definitely felt like it was. If not for magic, she'd be out of this cell, gone from this building. If not for Marley's dark magic, she wouldn't be here in the first place.

After a final look at Marley, Nasal advanced toward Zasha with a muzzle held out in front of him. At his approach, she snapped open her eyes.

The muzzle was made of thick, scarred leather, suggesting she hadn't been the only one unfortunate enough to end up on the other side of it. She didn't think her wolf would be able to pry it open.

As if Zasha were possessed of a contagious disease Nasal was concerned he'd catch, he slipped the muzzle over her mouth and jumped back.

She growled deep in her belly and wished like hell she could snap at him and make him piss himself. But she couldn't. Marley hadn't loosened his magical grip on her in the least. Now, he turned and smirked at Nasal, gesturing with his head for the man to get on with it already.

Nasal bit his lip, nodded nervously, and stepped forward again, sliding the harness around her ears and clasping the muzzle in place beneath her jaw. Then he tightened the front of the muzzle via another strap.

He stepped back. "That should be good enough." But he didn't sound sure, and one glance at Marley and the bandages that partially concealed his face had Nasal reaching into the deep, wide pockets of his cargo pants and withdrawing a zip-tie. He wrapped it between the two leather straps on her muzzle and cinched it tight—too tight. It hurt, cutting into her flesh.

Zasha added to her mental list of retributions: cinch a zip-tie too tightly on Nasal before she killed him so he would know what it felt like.

Next Nasal dug deep into his other pocket and came out with another zip-tie, this one longer.

Rounding her body, he ducked, more confident now that she was muzzled, and wrapped the zip-tie around her hind legs, cinching it tightly with an audible *ziipppp*.

Nasal joined Marley near the doorway and asked, "You still got 'er?"

Marley nodded, his eyes spelling out bloody murder despite his silence.

Zasha had no doubts about the kind of things he'd try to do to her if Boss Man didn't have a vested interest in her.

"All right," Nasal said. "Let's go, then. The first match is probably almost over. I doubt the guy lasted long. He was DT'ing pretty hard before he even went through the change. I doubt he made it more than a minute before Black Rack killed 'im."

Marley whipped his head toward the door and rolled his eyes a bit, suggesting they could be on their way if Nasal would just shut up.

Nasal got the message, proving he wasn't nearly as dense as Zasha assumed they all must be. Why else would anyone work for someone like Boss? She didn't figure anyone of any moderate intelligence and strength would willingly choose a life like this one, and all of the men seemed competent enough, so why hadn't they run themselves? Could it just be about the money? Surely no one's heart was that black...

But even as she thought it, she remembered how

her father had warned her how easily the hearts of men—and women—were corrupted.

Then she thought no longer about the *why*, and only directed her attention to the *how*. How was she going to survive this fight? How was she getting out of here? After she was out, she'd figure out how she'd get her real self back ... if there was any getting her back.

Marley used his magic to float her along the bleak hallway in front of him while Nasal brought up the rear, content to put as much distance between her and him as he could without appearing over-the-top cowardly.

They didn't bother to close the door behind them, nor had they bothered to shut several more doors that hung ajar as they moved farther along the wide hallway.

Zasha counted six open doors—no, wait, there were more.

Marley hovered her toward a turn in the hallway, and when they rounded it, her blood threatened to curdle despite the way her heartbeat was picking up speed.

Down this way, there were at least another six open doors.

Rank, sour odors spilled out of all of them, but

the smells were worse the closer they drew to the stairs at the end of the hallway.

As if the prisoners within them had been held captive within these cells for longer.

Nasal whistled as they passed the final open door. "The boss brought Wild Killer out to play. He must see a lot of potential in this bitch." Then he snorted, laughing at his own private joke. "More like the boss has a hard-on for all the money their fight's gonna fetch 'im. Wild Killer hasn't fought in a while, after that last fight damn near saw his leg ripped off at the hip. But for him to come out now? And to fight a bitch to boot when no girls ever fight…?" He whistled again, making Zasha rankle. Not that it did her any good.

"Glad we picked 'er up now, aren't you?" Nasal asked Marley, who whipped his head around too fast, obviously causing him pain. His eyes watered and his nostrils flared, his wrath temporarily directed from Zasha to his chatty companion.

"Damn, Marley. I forgot, okay? You don't gotta get all pissed. I didn't do nothing. I forgot 'cause I wasn't around to see her attack you."

And from the wistful tone of his voice at the end, he sounded like he would have very much liked to watch that.

Marley shot him the evil eye, and Nasal finally shut up.

It was just as well. Zasha had already started to tune him out, wanting to absorb everything she could about her surroundings. If she survived this fight—no, make that *when* she survived this fight—she'd have to know the route out of here.

Marley led her up some plain cement stairs, confirming her suspicions that they'd been underground. But then he just kept on climbing. Three flights later, and she realized they'd been very, very deep underground.

Where no one could hear their screams, she realized with sudden clarity.

She was just one of many in an ongoing operation. They needed to keep their activities secret from the police force, which wasn't great at attending to the issues of the residents of Flaming Arrow in general, but she didn't think even they would be able to look the other way if they discovered this kind of business was being run right beneath their noses.

Well, assuming she was still in Flaming Arrow. With a start, she realized she couldn't be certain even of that. She'd been unconscious when they transported her. They could, in theory, be almost anywhere.

Her spirit and hopes threatened to sink as she

wondered what kind of chances she had that her uncles would ever find her.

But then Marley led her along another long hallway, this one bordered by a wall marred by irregular scratches on one side, and cages enclosed by thick metal bars on the other.

The first three cells were empty.

"Guess the first three matches are done," Nasal said. "We took longer getting this bitch than I thought." He chuckled under his breath. "Or the kids gave out faster than I expected."

As if something like that could ever be funny. She was going to set fire to the entire place, and do her best to trap the men inside so they all burned with it.

At the fourth cell, Marley slowed and turned Zasha so she could see better, since once more her range of motion was limited. She could move some though, unlike before, and her gaze couldn't help but fall on the gigantic, snarling, vicious wolf enclosed behind bars.

When Nasal attempted to walk between Zasha's wolf and the cage, the larger wolf jumped at the bars. He was all teeth and dripping saliva, all deadly threats and horrible snarls.

Even as the bars singed his fur.

He slid his jaws through the bars, ignoring the

way they burned the shorter fur there, and snapped at Nasal, who squeaked and jumped backward.

Zasha didn't want to be scared. If ever there was a time to be brave, it was then. To win a tough fight, you have to have balls the size of a bull's, her Uncle Lev used to say while cupping an empty hand in front of him and scrunching up his face, totally unconcerned by the fact that she'd never have balls. She'd known what he meant.

You had to have courage to put yourself out there and take the risks necessary to win. If you lacked courage, it ultimately didn't matter how skilled you were, eventually someone was going to take you down, and then you'd be too scared to ever get back up again.

Unable to avoid staring into the wolf's wild violet eyes that vibrated with his fury, she understood that she'd have to pull courage from every hidden place she could source it, need to show up and give the fight with this beast her all.

Though she hadn't been able to get a fully accurate sense of her dimensions since she hadn't been able to examine her reflection, she thought she was probably at least fifty pounds lighter than he, and he was pure muscle. So was she, but that much muscle mass difference was important.

In the ring, when she was human, one look at an

opponent that outweighed her, and was this much larger, would have told her she had to be far more agile and faster than he was. Since most fighters were larger than she, this was usually the case, and yet she won most of her fights. She was nimble and good at outmaneuvering her opponent, sizing him up and sneaking into his weak spots while wearing him down. But this wolf didn't seem like he had any weak spots. And she doubted she'd be faster than him. She'd only just shifted into this body. There was no way she'd mastered it enough to outmaneuver this wolf.

His muscles rippled as he cycled through his desire to pummel the two men into mush. Strength radiated off him like heat. And when she scented the air, there wasn't one speck of fear coming from him, though there was something else there she couldn't identify. Some substance that felt foreign to the wolf.

Once more, despair threatened to overcome her, and briefly she wondered if she'd be able to find sufficient courage to face the wolf in the ring.

He snarled and growled some more, and finally threw his head back and howled. Though she might be new to this form, she recognized a battle cry when she heard it. It was too loud for the small, confined space, loud enough to vibrate against the walls.

Several other howls answered his call.

Devastation slammed into her. What was this place that they could hold so many strong wolves?

But then she felt the wolf's attention alight on her, and she realized none of his rage was directed at her.

In his eyes, she recognized desperation ... and compassion.

He didn't wish their circumstances on her any more than she would wish them on him.

He fought to survive only. To live.

Unlike the men and wizards, he didn't enjoy what he was forced to do. She read all of it in the depths of his pain.

"Save it for the ring," Nasal finally told Wild Killer, though his voice trembled slightly. "You'll get to have at her soon enough."

Nasal laughed nervously, then told Marley: "Come on, man. Enough. The boss wants her out there next. Hurry it up."

After a slight hesitation, during which Zasha thought Marley's delay was solely so Nasal understood Marley didn't take orders from him, he led Zasha farther down the hall.

Nasal walked ahead, pushing open a large door within a set of double doors, and held the one open.

Immediately, the scents of death, fear, and lots of people assaulted her.

Everywhere, strident sounds of shuffling, mumbling, and shouting people assailed her hearing. Squinting after the darkness of her underground prison, she attempted to make out what lay ahead of her under the sudden brightness of several large overhead spotlights.

She discovered herself inside a large arena, stands lining it on three sides. A large, thick metal fence, too tall to jump or climb in any form, separated her from the hundreds of people who filled the stands, excitement and anticipation wafting off them. Greed and lust too. Sweat and money. It sickened her.

She was busy wishing they'd all die as a voice called out through a surround-sound system.

"Ladies and gentlemen, the Pound always keeps you entertained. As usual, the Pound won't disappoint." His intonation was that of an entertainer. "Next for you we have the fight you've all been waiting for. Wicked Woman versus Wild Killer!"

Excited murmurs swept across the crowd before the people roared.

"That's right, ladies and gents. Today, the Pound presents our very first fight where the wolf is a female!"

"What about Black Rack?" someone yelled from the audience.

"Wicked Woman isn't like Black Rack. She isn't like Wild Killer either. Wicked Woman was made by magic. The Pound presents to you the first ever magic-made wolf woman in a fight!"

A hush settled across the crowd before it erupted. Hooting, cheering, and clapping devastated the silence.

"Fast now," Marley garbled to Nasal.

Then Marley was setting Zasha down on a hard-packed dirt surface, and Nasal whipped beneath her legs with a knife.

She almost wished his hand would slip and he'd accidentally end her. She didn't want to take any part in whatever this was.

But no, like Wild Killer, she was a survivor, and she couldn't wholeheartedly wish for her end to arrive any sooner than it must.

Nasal sliced through the zip-tie holding her hind legs together, through the one clamping shut her jaws, unleashing a torrent of tingles from the too-tight bindings. Then he tucked away the blade and unclasped both buckles on her harness.

Without a word, Nasal backed through the door they'd exited, and Marley soon followed.

Only once they closed, bolted, and threw a bar of some sort behind the two doors to keep them shut,

Marley dropped the one hand that kept his spell trained on her.

She regained her ability to move, and even as her thoughts stampeded out of control, attempting to consider all the what-ifs, she began to move her body, loosening up for the fight of her life.

It might well be the last one.

CHAPTER SIX
ZASHA

ZASHA HADN'T PAID attention to the other single door set farther down the wall until it slammed open, colliding with the wall behind it, where her keen eyes picked up on a deep groove in the cinder block of the wall, suggesting this same thing had happened many times before. Before the door could begin to swing shut of its own momentum, Wild Killer burst through the opening, turning to snap at the people behind him even as he advanced.

She couldn't contain the snarl that rumbled through her when she noticed the one man who'd been there on the night of her capture, the sole one of the four she hadn't managed to injure in some way, was pressing a cattle prod to Wild Killer's hindquarters.

The wolf was in the middle of lunging for the

man, who wore running sneakers, but still had no chance of being fast enough to outrun the wolf, when the man shoved the prod into his belly, holding down the button that streamed electric current through the electrodes at the tip of the club for several moments too long.

The wolf finally sagged as the electricity vibrated through him, flopping onto the same hard-packed dirt she stood on.

The man spat on the ground next to the wolf's heaving body and snarled, "Stupid fucking wolf," as if he had every right to be angry.

That hot stick had been rigged to deliver more voltage than a stun gun.

Zasha waged a brief battle with her instincts. Part of her wanted to rush to Wild Killer's side to aid him. The jackass brute in the running shoes had juiced him up enough to kill an ordinary human. Another part of her, the part that still wanted to believe she was human, warned her not to approach the enraged, dangerous wolf. Sure, he was down now, but she'd bet he wouldn't be down for long. A survivor like him wouldn't allow it. Besides, she didn't know what she could do to help. She couldn't speak; she was an animal. That one thought rocketed through her, leaving her stunned.

She hadn't had the time to process what had

happened to her, much less what it all might mean in the long run. As far as her captors were concerned, there would be no long run for her.

She realized the crowd was cheering, and she couldn't stop herself from releasing a deep, low growl up in their direction.

A few laughs erupted throughout the crowd.

They were *laughing* at her. They were laughing that she dared oppose their cruel treatment.

Their voices slid across the mostly filled stands, but she didn't bother straining to distinguish them and decipher what they were saying. She knew what kind of things they'd be shouting. Just the thought of it made her expand her vow to burn down the place—with them inside it too. She'd be doing the world a favor.

Still uncertain what to do, Zasha found herself moving. Cautiously, she approached the wolf.

"Look at Wicked Woman," the announcer said over the speaker system with a husky chuckle. "She's smarter than we thought. She's going to take Wild Killer out before he's even standing. That's against the rules, Wicked Woman. You have to wait until I announce the start of the fight."

But the announcer didn't seem invested in what he said. Zasha suspected he hoped she would attack the wolf while he was down and give him something to talk about.

She continued her slow approach, and when she drew within a body's length of the wolf, he snarled at her, his chest heaving beneath thick, dark gray fur. His violet eyes blazed and threatened her as they pinned her in their stare.

She chuffed and, certain he couldn't lunge at her quite yet, drew to his side. When he snapped at empty air with deadly jaws, she paused to glare at him.

"Oh boy," the announcer said. "She has him at her mercy. Will she break all the rules and take the kill shot right now?"

Excited rumbles reached them from the stands, and Zasha worked to tune out the announcer even as he was offering her another half-hearted reminder that she was supposed to wait.

Zasha moved toward the wolf's hindquarters, and he snapped at her again. But she saw resignation in his eyes.

Prod had zapped him so thoroughly that it was a wonder the wolf's insides weren't liquefied. The scent of singed hair and flesh thickly coated the air around the wolf.

Panting weakly, the wolf actually thought she was going to kill him, just as the announcer predicted. She wished she could talk to him and tell him they didn't have to give any of these pricks what they wanted. Maybe they could band together and kill them all—once he could move again.

She also wondered at Boss' intentions. Had he told Prod to weaken the wolf so fully that he couldn't fight back? Zasha doubted much happened in this arena without Boss' orders.

The wolf settled his snarls, and when she met his violet eyes, he gave her a single nod.

She stilled. He'd just given her permission to end him. To put a finish to his torment as a captive.

She scoffed, nudged one of his limp paws away, and licked the open wound on his thigh, the flesh where the man had pressed the cattle prod to him—probably not for the first time, she came to think; he would've probably had to motivate Wild Killer to leave his cell when the wolf knew what awaited him. How much electricity had run through the wolf's body?

She licked his thigh again, and the wolf stiffened. She ran her big, long tongue over him again, unsure exactly why she was doing it, only that she should. The flesh was the screaming red of raw flesh in some parts, and charred in others. She continued licking.

When she felt the wolf's stare on her, she looked up, still cleaning his wound. His violet eyes held emotion of some sort beyond the rage and promises for vengeance she'd seen in them before, but she didn't understand what exactly.

Then the voice of the announcer filtered through to her once more, and she realized it was because he was suddenly agitated. A glance up told her why.

Boss crowded the announcer, towering over the smaller man, whispering urgently at him.

The announcer squeaked and the microphone he gripped in an iron hold caught the sound, even though he held it away from their mouths.

The audience hushed, their attention finally off of Zasha and the other wolf, and on one of the most dangerous predators inside the arena.

Her sights pinned on Boss Man, Zasha nudged the wolf with the dark gray fur, hoping he'd receive her message.

She wanted to say, "Get up. Get up before they come kill you for not fighting me!"

Once he was up, maybe they could figure out a way for them both to leave the arena with their lives. Though maybe not. She was under no illusion that this crowd would be satisfied by anything less than violence and bloodshed, and Boss relied on their satisfaction for his continued business.

Dammit, she didn't know what to do!

"Oh wow, ladies and gents," the announcer said

in an enthusiastic rush that couldn't quite conceal his nervousness at Boss Man's proximity. "Do we have a surprise for you today!"

His voice rang out through the large arena with its tall ceiling, reaching up maybe thirty feet, but it lacked that smooth whiskey feel all public announcers were supposed to possess.

"You know the Pound never lets you down. What's better than a fight between two wolves?" He paused, drawing out the suspense. "How about a fight between three wolves?" the announcer cried out, doing his best to rile up his audience.

He succeeded.

"And what's better than a fight between three dogs than a ... *cat fiiight*?" He sang out the last bit, and laughter rang out in the stands before hoots and hollers of encouragement followed. "That's right, ladies and gents, we're going to have a bitch fight, brought to you by the Pound and your mystery sponsor." He glanced at Boss Man with theatrical slyness, making Zasha wonder how his identity could be a mystery when he was standing right there.

Applause thundered from the bleachers. But Boss Man just stood next to the announcer, taking it all in as if he barely cared.

The cheering transformed into a standing ovation, and Zasha thought she might actually be sick to her stomach and throw up all the gruel and murky water she'd ingested since she was kidnapped.

When the announcer called out, "Bring out Blaaack Raaaaaaack!" Zasha snapped her attention to Wild Killer's violet eyes. This time, she could read them easily: disappointment, despair, and fury. He wasn't any happier about Black Rack's inclusion in this hideous charade than she was.

She nudged him with her nose, encouraging him to stand. Whoever this Black Rack was, she was a true werewolf or wolf shifter like he was, which meant she'd likely be as fierce and strong as him.

Zasha had no idea how Black Rack would behave once in the arena with them, but she doubted she could count on her to take it easy on either of them. Not that Zasha was responsible for Wild Killer's fate. But even so, no fighter worth her weight would attack someone while they were incapacitated. That was dishonorable, and despite all the colorful tidbits of sometimes questionable wisdom her father and uncles imparted on her, they had consistently taught her about honor.

Your integrity is one of the few things in this life that is all your own, my volchok, her dad would say, speaking one of the few words in his native language he ever used with her. It was an endearment he reserved for her alone.

Her uncles all echoed his sentiment in their own way.

Zasha had absorbed this teaching and taken it to heart. Especially now, she might not have control over much, but she would always have control over her choices and her actions. She refused to hurt a wolf who was so injured he could barely move.

But this Black Rack? Well, she would be a different story.

Zasha didn't want to injure anyone in any permanent way beyond the people responsible for putting them in this ring. But if Black Rack came at her and tried to kill her? Yeah, she'd fight back; you bet she would.

"Bring out Blaaack Raaaaack!" the announcer called out while Boss moved away from him and toward a VIP box, where a couple of young women waited for him, wearing garments that melded the line between dress and bikini.

While the audience waited for Black Rack to enter the arena, the announcer filled the time.

"You'll remember, ladies and gents, that these fights are to the death." He laughed arrogantly, and Zasha cursed the high fences that separated her from him. If he laughed at their predicament just one more time, or if she had to hear him say "ladies and gents" again...

"*Of course* you remember the fights are to the death," he continued. "That's why you're here. Because there's nothing that makes you feel quite as alive as witnessing death, am I right?"

"Hell yeah," a woman called to him from the stands, and several others mimicked her cry.

Beside Zasha, Wild Killer sighed, as if he were as disappointed in these depraved individuals as she was.

"That's right, ladies and gents," the announcer said and chuckled again.

Zasha growled.

"In this unique fight of three wolves, we'll have not one death, but *two deaths*! The last wolf standing will be our winner. Now, we know you already placed your bets for one fight, but given that Wild Killer has apparently decided to lie down and die, we're going to void all bets on the fight between him and Wicked Woman."

A few complaints rumbled through the stands, but the announcer silenced them with an uplifted hand, back to acting confident now that Boss wasn't crowding him.

"Now, now. I'm sure you'll all agree that the Pound is giving you an even better fight now. So grab the girls coming your way … and place your new bets."

Laughter swept the crowd once more as a man with a big gut and a comb-over took the announcer's instructions literally and grabbed the ass of the nearest girl, giving it a loud smack. The girl, who appeared in her late teens or early twenties, didn't seem surprised in the least, and when the man pulled her into his lap, she let him.

Zasha snarled on the girl's behalf, recognizing that there were several victims in this arena.

"Come on, ladies and gents! Place your bets before Black Rack enters the ring," the speaker warned. "She's coming soon." He laughed again, twisting his words into a lewd suggestion.

Then the announcer dropped the mic to his side, and received a bottle of water from yet another girl. Zasha realized there was a whole staff of these scantily clad girls who were barely women.

A few minutes passed while the men and the few women in the audience clamored to place their bets. Meanwhile, Zasha finally stepped away from Wild Killer, the worst of his wounds cleaned, and proceeded to watch him warily.

Though he continued to lie on his side, she could tell he'd recovered quite a bit. His breathing was no longer shallow, and his eyes seemed clearer, making her realize that they'd been clouded before. She suspected he could stand now, but wasn't choosing to in the same way that she'd opted to rest earlier to heal faster.

She didn't think he could best her in a fight just yet, but she suspected he was stronger than he appeared at this point, suggesting that the rumors about werewolves were true, and they did heal far faster than human beings did.

A howl split the air from somewhere behind the wall next to them, and Zasha knew it was Black Rack. She just knew. That howl spoke to the wolf part of her. Though she didn't understand what all of it meant, she felt her wolf ready for battle. But her wolf wanted to join Black Rack in her call to fight, not challenge her.

"Oh boy," the announcer said, bringing the mic to his mouth again. "That's Black Rack, and she sounds *angry*. You have one more minute to place your bets, and then the she-wolf will be in the ring and then no more bets."

Wild Killer staggered to his feet, wobbling for a moment, before remaining upright. Zasha looked at him with a questioning gaze that he met with one of his own. Something meaningful was happening in their exchange, but she'd be damned if she knew what it was. She sensed that she was supposed to better understand the unspoken messages between them, but she didn't comprehend much about her wolf form.

He whined at her, and she didn't think it was meant to sound like a whine. No, he was definitely talking to her, his ears twitching while he waited for her response.

She didn't know what to do, so she whined back, imitating his pitch, hoping like hell she didn't just tell him to sniff her butt or something.

His ears twitched some more, but Zasha didn't know if she'd managed to communicate with him at all. Principally, she didn't know what she would say to him if she could. They were trapped unless one of them died. And there was no way to get to anyone in the audience, much less into Boss' VIP box, which was even higher off the ground than the stands. All of them were protected by a thick metal chain-link fence that climbed halfway up to the ceiling and its obnoxious spotlights that warmed her fur to uncomfortable levels. Despite the distance, the light bulbs were large, and trained on them.

The same door that had released Wild Killer swung open another time, and Black Rack launched out of it. No cattle prod necessary, she bounded into the arena, processing her surroundings in seconds. She flicked a look at Zasha, then at Wild Killer, then her audience, and then Zasha again.

Black Rack stalked between Zasha and Wild Killer, stepping between them, and lowered into her haunches, baring her teeth at Zasha.

Wild Killer whined at Black Rack in that way he had with Zasha, and Zasha tried to imitate him, still unsure what she was trying to communicate. At that point it was anything that would help Black Rack realize that there had to be another way, that she was in the same boat as the two of them. She might not be a true werewolf, or wolf shifter or whatever, but she'd been transformed into a wolf just the same. They weren't enemies—at least, they shouldn't be. They didn't have to be.

But Black Rack visibly shook off Wild Killer's message, and didn't even pay attention to hers, whatever her nonsensical communication turned out to be.

Black Rack had thick fur the color of a rich, dark chocolate, and her teeth flashed a bright ivory in stark contrast to the hue of her fur. She was smaller than Wild Killer, but not by much, which definitely made her larger than Zasha, who guessed Black Rack had at least twenty-five pounds of muscle on her. A distinct advantage in this form that Zasha barely knew how to use.

Then Zasha thought no more, at least not in any way that she noticed. Without warning and without any kind of signal from the announcer, Black Rack charged.

Gasps and squeals of excitement peppered the bleachers above them. In the split second before Black Rack reached her, Zasha registered only one thing: this wolf planned to kill her.

And it seemed the only way to stop her was to kill her first.

Zasha cleared her mind of any ideas of fear, embraced the readiness of her instincts, and coiled her muscles.

She'd trained to fight all her life.

Zasha was a warrior.

And warriors overcame ... until they died.

If this was her day to die, then Zasha would give the fight everything she had left.

She bared her teeth at the other wolf and waited for the right moment to jump out of the way, then circle the other wolf, and pounce.

CHAPTER SEVEN

QUANNAH

AFTER CHOKING OUT TWO BURLY, well-dressed bodyguards, Quannah and five of the strongest wolf shifters of the Smoky Mountain Pack prepared to slip through the entrance of an unpretentious building on the outskirts of the city of Flaming Arrow.

Quannah was grateful for the two overly muscled men, whose bulk prevented them from moving fast enough to resist the pack's swift attack. If not for their presence, he might not have found the building he suspected held three of their own somewhere in its depths.

The pack's alpha, Corin, had been searching for the underground wolf fighting ring since some dark mages had taken three of their members when they were scouting some wolves who were new to the area for potential inclusion in the Smoky Mountain Pack. But despite Corin allotting much of the pack's resources to locating their missing members, the fighting ring wasn't easy to find. For nearly six months, Quannah and others had searched without reward.

Quannah was Corin's beta and second-in-command, the only wolf Corin entrusted with a mission as important as this one. And though Quannah was eager to find the Pound, with its horrific name that made reference to equally horrific dog fights, because his alpha ordered it, he was also invested because the wolves that had been snatched were his friends—*family*.

And the Smoky Mountain Pack was a family. Though under Corin's command, either you held your own or you couldn't be a part of their pack of wolves.

It wasn't because Corin was unusually hard-hearted, it was because Corin had taken it upon himself to battle the hunters—and put them out of business once and for all.

For as long as werewolves existed, among the humans there were those who hunted their kind. The wolves referred to those who pursued them simply as the hunters, and did everything they could to avoid them. The hunters might be human, but their weapons were not of the human world.

To fight the hunters wasn't a new purpose. The alpha before Corin had done the same, as had the alpha before him. To be a member of the Smoky Mountain Pack was to be a fighter. A warrior.

Every wolf understood that coming in; it was why Corin was so rigorous in his selection. And so the Smoky Mountain Pack trod a dangerous line. The wolves—wolf shifters, who could transform at will, and werewolves, who were tied to the rhythms of the moon—sought to remain unnoticed by the humans, but mostly to avoid the unwanted attention of the hunters ... until the wolves could flip the tables.

They would be the hunters. *They* would be the predators seeking out their prey.

Corin had sworn to his pack that the wolves wouldn't have to run and hide much longer, that he would carve out a safe world for their kind, where they wouldn't have to fear persecution for being what they were—something they had no control over.

As a rule, Corin forbade them from exposing themselves unnecessarily. Yes, much of the world was aware that werewolves existed—though they didn't often differentiate them from wolf shifters—and even those who weren't fully aware heard the rumors and whispers. Corin didn't necessarily want to conceal their existence, he just didn't want to draw attention to their particular pack or its location.

Corin Gray Wolf prioritized the safety of his pack above all else, and so they skirted through the world beyond the boundaries of their land as if they were shadows or ghosts, doing what they could not to draw much attention to themselves.

But not today. Not now. Not when Quannah might finally have a bead on their missing friends. Sure, they'd do their best not to be noticed, but they'd return the wolves to their pack—at any cost.

Earlier that day, one of their wolves, Cassie, had driven over to Flaming Arrow, via a circuitous route meant to throw off anyone watching, to run some errands for the pack. As a rule, the pack avoided venturing beyond its home territory any more than necessary. Its wolves remained safe so long as their location remained secret. Besides, the rundown and broken city held little interest to them. Which was why Cassie, who was one of the lower ranking members of the pack, had been assigned the task. None of them enjoyed traveling to the city, where storefronts were dingy and depressing. But it was still the closest major city to their territory, and so it was where they came to stock up on provisions they couldn't get elsewhere —like soap and hops. The lowest ranking wolves always jostled over who would have to make the trip.

For once, however, the entire pack was excited by the results of Cassie's trip to the city. She'd been walking through the streets during early afternoon—because even the wolves knew you didn't visit Flaming Arrow on your own when it was dark unless you were asking for trouble—when she'd turned down Market Alley for one last purchase and a man she'd never seen before had reached out of a dark doorway and grabbed her wrist.

Cassie, though relatively new to the pack, was no weakling. This man who grabbed Cassie identified what she was, probably because of the violet streaks in her eyes, but he apparently hadn't realized that while she was a slender, slight woman, she possessed strength far greater than her size. And she didn't appreciate being grabbed—by anybody.

When she had him pinned on the sidewalk, regardless of a few curious passersby, he rushed to tell her he'd been waiting for a wolf, that he had information she would want.

She eased up on the knee to his neck and listened ... and heard enough to call Quannah.

Two hours later, Quannah, with a wad of cash in his pocket, met up with Cassie, who'd tucked the informant away in a darkened alley. The man's hair was stringy and greasy, making it appear darker than it probably was. The flesh beneath his eyes was too dark for his skin, and he licked his lips continuously, obviously a nervous gesture. When Quannah forked over the cash, greed glittered in the man's eyes, and he sang like a canary.

The man, who refused to supply his name, worked in a secret lab that processed drugs. This, on its own, wasn't noteworthy news. The streets of Flaming Arrow crawled with dangerous drugs and the people using them.

It was the kind of drugs this lab was creating that held Quannah's interest.

The drugs were meant to subdue werewolves, the man said, licking his lips and eyeing Quannah. Tall, muscular, and agile in the way of a true predator, most people were cautious around him. Quannah was used to it. Even among the wolves, he often received a similar reaction.

"What else do the drugs do?" he pushed the informant.

"Keep them from changing when they want to. Keep them from healing real fast."

"Does it interfere with their pack link?"

The man nodded, his greasy hair sliding around his head in clumps.

For six months, Quannah had reached out to

their wolves via the pack link and sent out queries in every direction, letting the right people know that the Smoky Mountain Pack was in the market for the location of their three missing wolves. Until now, no one had heard a thing, which in itself was odd. It wasn't easy to hide three wolves, especially not the three wolves that had been snatched. They were some of the pack's toughest, and they would have fought whoever took them with lethal force.

The informant hadn't been able to tell Quannah much more about the drug, which he called Wolf Woofer—an insultingly cartoonish moniker. But he'd known where he delivered the drugs, which made the price for his information worthwhile all on its own.

"The place where we drop off the drugs changes all the time," the informant told Quannah. "And it's never me that does the delivering. But this last time the usual guy wasn't around, so they asked me to do it. Told me the place to take it, and I took it. That's all I know."

After confirming the man didn't know anything more that could help him, Quannah sent him off and led Cassie away from Market Alley and to their cars, anxious to move on this information.

If the delivery location was different every time, it meant either that the wolves were moved often, or that the dropoff was changed to keep people away from the Pound's true location.

Quannah couldn't even be sure that this Wolf Woofer drug had anything to do with their missing wolves, but his gut told him it did. And even if it hadn't, it was the only lead they had.

A quick call to Corin with an update, the alpha sent two cars full of their wolves to meet him and Cassie. While they completed the two-hour drive to Flaming Arrow, Quannah and Cassie scouted out the delivery location ... and got lucky.

They trailed the two bodyguards to a building large enough to house an operation of the Pound's rumored scope.

With the bodyguards now two unconscious lumps on the ground, it was time to move. One of the wolves, Lucian, frisked them for radios, grabbed them, and passed them off to Flynn, who would wait in the cars outside with some of the wolves.

Flynn was the pack's third-in-command—the gamma—and though he was extremely capable and an excellent choice to enter the Pound to rescue their wolves—assuming they were there—they didn't know what they were walking into, nor how likely it was that they'd be recognized for what they were. Having someone like Flynn, and more wolves tucked away as a backup plan was smart.

Also smart would have been to do some reconnaissance of the place and how it did business. Quannah always did things the measured way; it was the best way to survive in a world like theirs. But they didn't have time for any of that. This was the first time they'd been able to pinpoint the Pound's location, and if not for those two bodyguards protecting an entrance so rundown and lackluster that it didn't look like it needed security, they still might not have found it.

No, they couldn't afford to let their wolves slip away.

It was difficult to become a part of the Smoky Mountain Pack, and you had to earn your place within its ranks. But once you did, the others would fight for you until the end.

If this was their only chance at getting their three wolves back, then it was worth the risk of moving in without sufficient information. And if the risk didn't pay off and Quannah went down, then Flynn would be left behind to fill his space in the pack hierarchy.

Quannah nodded at Flynn, and Flynn nodded back, everything that was left unsaid between them nonetheless understood. Then Quannah studied the five wolves who were to accompany him inside, while Flynn signaled to some of the wolves that were to remain behind to help him hide the bodies of the bodyguards.

The men Quannah had chosen to come with him wouldn't hesitate to do whatever needed to be done once they were inside. "Remember," he whispered to them, "once we're through that door, no speaking. Not even a whisper when you think no one's around. We have no idea what we're walking into. Pack link only. Stick together and watch each other's backs. Let's leave here in one piece and with our missing wolves."

Quannah met eyes with every one of the men. Though the eyes sat in radically different faces, they were all a shade of violet, though in some the plum color was less noticeable, which allowed those wolves to blend with humans more than the others.

Which prompted Quannah to say: "Hide your eyes, unless it's worse to do that."

Not even contact lenses fully concealed the violet glow of their eyes.

Then Quannah slid the door open silently and slipped inside, holding it ajar until the five wolves followed. Then they stilled, allowing their sharp sight to adjust to the dim lighting, and, at least for Quannah, for the varying rancid scents to roll through him. There were the typical female perfumes that he hated, their artificial fragrances all but nauseating to him. But then there were even worse smells: death, blood, and fear.

He shook his head, signaling nothing in particular other than an outlet for his mounting anger, and stalked quietly down a wide, dimly lit hallway, keeping his ears and nose on the alert. If this was indeed the Pound, then they were bound to encounter people.

He didn't remind his men to stay sharp; they knew.

When the long hallway ended and allowed for a turn in either direction, he debated. They could split up or they could stay together. Another of the reasons he left Flynn and some of the wolves outside was because he didn't want to draw unnecessary attention to their numbers. He doubted the gamblers arrived at the Pound in big posses.

Quickly, he made a decision. Through their link, and limiting his message just to the wolves inside the building with him—an ability only he and the alpha possessed—he said: *Lucian and Nolan, you're with me. Silver, Webb, and Dax, you stick together. No separating.*

Quannah took a left with the two men close on his heels, Silver led the others right.

The long hall in front of Quannah took another turn before opening into a large foyer with bathrooms off both sides. Gone was the dingy dankness, replaced by opulence that didn't belong in an unidentified industrial building.

As the three men passed, two women, dressed in bodycon, stilettos, and bright makeup, stepped out of the restroom, giggling at something the taller blonde said over her shoulder to the shorter brunette, whose tits were bursting from her dress.

The brunette's attention landed on the men first, and the blonde quickly followed her friend's gaze, saying, "Well, well, where'd you hotties come from?"

"Yeah," the brunette said. "You're fiii-ine."

Lucian, you take the blonde. Nolan, the brunette, Quannah said.

Immediately, the two men flanking Quannah shot the women grins that screamed sex, momentarily freezing them in place. Quannah was continually amazed at how easy it was to sway women to thoughts of sex, overpowering their good sense. Humans said the men were the ones who thought of sex all the time, but it was his experience that women did just the same.

Like any good wolf, Lucian and Nolan knew how to work the advantages they had. Right then, if they had to lead the women to believe they were about to have a very fun evening with some very hot men, then so be it. This way, they wouldn't scream and alert anyone to their presence.

Lucian grinned until dimples formed on his cheeks, then bent to whisper in the blonde's ear. Nolan was working a similar move, and moments later the men had both women in sleeper chokeholds, one arm wrapped around their necks, the other pressed to the back of their heads. No matter how much their eyes bulged, with their necks pressed against the men's bulging forearms and biceps, the women couldn't scream as the blood flow to their brains slowed.

It was one of the first moves any new member of the Smoky Mountain Pack learned, and it was one they kept handy in their arsenal. The move was effective and, when done correctly, didn't leave lasting damage.

Ringed by eye shadow, the women's eyes eventually closed, and their heads slumped forward. Without Quannah having to tell them, Lucian and Nolan checked their pulses to make sure they were steady, scooped the women up so as not to risk leaving any telling marks of struggle on the polished marble floor, and walked them back into the bathroom. They'd bind their hands, feet, and mouths with the zip-ties and tape, tuck them into a stall, and lock the door.

When the men emerged, Quannah said: *Clock's ticking now*.

Sooner or later, someone would miss the women. From the way they were all dolled up, Quannah guessed it was going to be a very rich man who brought the two along as arm candy.

A sleeper chokehold usually knocked a person out for less than a minute—hence the zip-ties, tape, and hurried pace. They had to make the most of the time they had.

Beyond the grandiose foyer, and thankfully out of sight of the bathrooms, he spotted a concession stand, but not like those at sporting events. This stand offered champagne and hard drinks, caviar, and carved beef sandwiches with horseradish and tiny pickles.

"Welcome, sirs," a female attendant sang out at them in the trained tone of someone rewarded for their level of guest courtesy. "May I interest you in a drink?"

Though Quannah wanted to snap at the woman and ask how she could work at a place like this that condoned pointless death, appearances mattered while they could still slip under the radar.

Forcing calm he didn't feel, he turned to her. "No, but thank you very much."

Convinced by his good looks, and obviously not

focusing on the slight violet of his eyes, which his irises hid better than most, she smiled back at him.

"Well, you can page me if you change your mind. Each row of seats has a call button."

"I'll keep that in mind," he said before stalking off. The wealthy men who came here wouldn't pay her much mind, he reminded himself. And though they'd struggled to find the location of the Pound, they had managed to discover what it was about more easily: a gambling ring for the elite. Whispers had reached even the remote acreage that housed their pack. But garnering an invitation to the Pound was far trickier.

"Ladies and gents," a male's voice called out over a loudspeaker, "you're about to witness Pound history."

As Quannah walked toward the lights ahead of them, he felt Lucian and Nolan tense behind him.

So they'd finally found it. *The Pound*. With how lavish and extravagant the foyer was, he suspected this was their permanent location. They just moved around the spots of delivery for the drugs so no one would find out where they held the fights beyond those people they wanted to know.

Quannah reached a railing and stopped while Lucian and Nolan flanked him.

They emerged at the top of an indoor stadium,

lined with seats above an arena, where three wolves faced off.

Quannah tightened his fingers around the high-end polished walnut of the banister until it cracked. He forced himself to release his grip.

We found Kisha and Ty, Quannah announced via the pack link, extending the range of his message to the entire Smoky Mountain Pack, including his alpha. Even back at their compound, they'd hear him.

Two of their three missing wolves were in the center of the arena, below large fences, probably threaded with silver, that guaranteed the safety of the patrons.

And a third wolf, who should have been shitting herself facing down two of their pack's most ferocious wolves.

But wasn't.

She was preparing to attack.

CHAPTER EIGHT

QUANNAH

QUANNAH STARED down at the third wolf.

She was significantly smaller than Ty, hence the beta's assumption that she was a female, but she was also more petite than Kisha, and Kisha was one of the smallest in their entire pack of nearly four hundred—though she made up for what she lacked in size with attitude, of which she had plenty. Between the two of them, Ty and Kisha had at least a hundred pounds on the other wolf, probably more.

She should be cowering. Why wasn't she?

Rumors of how the Pound did its business had also reached their pack. They stole people from the streets and forced them to become wolves through dark spells. They altered a being's nature in the most unnatural of ways. He couldn't imagine a worse fate.

It wasn't often done, because it shouldn't be

done. Ever.

This wolf would be losing her mind if she was created by dark magic. She must be a recently turned werewolf instead, since she couldn't be a wolf shifter. Shifters were born, not made, and her movements, though sharper than he expected, were awkward in the way of pups before they got used to their limbs.

"Wow, ladies and gents," the announcer called over a loudspeaker, making Quannah, Lucian, and Nolan wince at the volume. "It looks like Black Rack and Wild Killer are banding together to take down Wicked Woman. That's not fair, now is it?" The man, who largely resembled a rat with shifty, beady eyes and an overbite, cackled. "Wicked Woman is a new wolf, just a day old. Black Rack and Wild Killer will rip her to shreds."

So she wasn't a werewolf. The moon was new.

The announcer's delight at the prospect of the new wolf's destruction rolled through the sound system, prompting Quannah to silently vow to kill him first.

As the audience reacted to the announcer's theatrics with a smattering of hollers and applause, Quannah trained his attention on their wolves. Was the announcer right? Were Ty and Kisha about to tear into the new wolf?

The Smoky Mountain Pack was renowned

among the supernatural community for the ferocity of its members. As a whole, they prided themselves on being tough, strong, and fully dedicated to their cause of taking down the hunters once and for all. But that ferocity wasn't cruelty. Ty and Kisha shouldn't attack a wolf who was at such a disadvantage, not unless it was in self-defense.

The fur of the other wolf was a color he'd never seen before: a mottled gray and ... almost a yellow peeking out from beneath the gray.

Despite her origins, there was no doubt her wolf had been created correctly. Muscle rippled beneath fur. Once she got the hang of her wolf body, she'd be strong for her size.

She wouldn't live long enough, however. No wolf made that way could.

She was crouched down into her haunches, her teeth bared, snarling at Ty and Kisha as they prowled, circling her. The wolf's eyes roved constantly, her body never still as she took in the enemy from all sides.

Quannah flared his nostrils. Ty and Kisha shouldn't be her enemies. None of this was right.

He could sense Lucian and Nolan at his sides waiting for his orders. Their plan hadn't extended much beyond getting in, grabbing their wolves, and getting out. Since they didn't know what they'd be walking into, it was the best they could do with the meager time they'd had to prepare. But neither of the men would prompt him. He'd commanded silence while they were inside, and though they were far enough away from the audience that it was likely no one would hear them, they would obey their beta's orders. Besides, though Quannah didn't see, smell, or hear anyone who might be able to eavesdrop, in the world of magic that didn't guarantee no one was there. If the Pound was converting wolves with the help of mages and their dark magic, then anything was possible within these walls.

The sooner they grabbed their wolves and got out, the better.

But he was struggling to take his eyes off the fight below. He didn't want the new wolf to die, and he didn't want Ty or Kisha to be the one to kill her.

But if they didn't kill her during the fight, the new wolf would just end up dying anyway, and probably after significant pain and torment. Maybe it was better that their wolves should kill her now and put her out of her misery. It would explain the behavior of their wolves, and why they seemed like they were ready to tear out the new wolf's throat.

Oh, but that wasn't true, Quannah noticed. Ty was holding back some, eyes pinned on Kisha instead of on the new wolf.

Which wasn't right. Ty had been born into their pack. He'd been trained for combat since the beginning. He would know better than to take his eyes from a threat.

Quannah felt Lucian and Nolan's energy push in on him from either side, meaning that they were actively waiting for him, expecting him to give an order right then. But he couldn't seem to look away from the scene unfolding beneath them, from the gray-and-yellow wolf.

If he left their perch to access the lower levels, would the she-wolf with that rare amber fur be dead the next time he saw her? That thought held him in place when it shouldn't.

Kisha lunged at the she-wolf, and the she-wolf dove out of the way just in time, spinning back toward her enemy faster than she should have been able to as a new wolf. She then thrust forward in an attack that almost managed to snip Kisha's hind leg.

Lucian tensed beside him as the she-wolf didn't pause, but rather whipped her head in the opposite direction, teeth first, and grazed Kisha's front leg.

Ty stood off to the side of both wolves, as if he couldn't decide whether to intervene, which wasn't like him, making Quannah suspect he was trying to determine which wolf to defend.

The pack bond was thicker than blood. No

matter what Kisha was or wasn't doing, Ty should be supporting her.

Quannah watched as Ty finally engaged in the fight, backing up Kisha, baring his teeth at the she-wolf. It was then that the overhead spotlights skimmed across Ty's injuries, the raw flesh reflecting light. One of his hindquarters and a large patch on his belly were bare of fur.

Nolan growled softly before silencing himself; he knew his friends were noticing the same thing.

Time to get Ty and Kisha out of there.

The audience was rapt as vicious snarls tore through the arena. Even the announcer seemed to momentarily forget he was supposed to be calling out the fight before he brought the microphone back to his lips to spew his nastiness.

Ty nipped at the she-wolf but didn't cause damage. Even hurt as he obviously was, he should have been able to take the she-wolf down.

When Ty nipped, Kisha swung around him and threw herself at the she-wolf, sinking her teeth into a front leg.

The she-wolf yelped, and as Kisha whipped her head to either side around her hold on the she-wolf's leg, inflicting maximum damage, the she-wolf did what prey didn't often do.

Instead of trying to minimize the damage on her

front leg, she slid her leg out to the side, ripping it out of Kisha's jaws.

Blood gushed from the open wound, red and gaping even from a distance, marring that odd yellow fur. The she-wolf had deepened her injuries.

But she had also gotten free, an end she probably wouldn't have achieved any other way.

Quannah felt the interest of the other two wolves beside him. That was a move one of them might pull, not an unsuspecting victim snatched from the streets and forced to become something they were never meant to be. Even odder, before Kisha could attack again, Ty rammed into her. Not hard enough to hurt her, but enough to interfere.

By the time Kisha spun to growl a warning at Ty, the she-wolf was on her feet, stalking the two of them as if half her front leg weren't hanging off the bone.

Lucian looked at Quannah, and the beta met the question in his friend's eyes.

But Quannah snapped out of it. They could figure out what was so odd about this she-wolf later. They had to move before someone noticed the bimbos in the bathroom missing and went searching for them. They had to take advantage of the fact that most everyone in the stands was now on their feet, peering down at the arena, fists clenched as they called out for more blood.

He should set the whole place on fire and rid the world of these diseased humans. They were all sick.

Come on, he told Lucian and Nolan through a limited pack link. *We need to get down there.*

He left off the rest of what he was thinking. How a part of him was wishing that their wolves would go ahead and kill the amber she-wolf.

He knew what it was like for new wolves. Their pack had several werewolves, most turned against their will. The confusion, desperation, and desolation they'd all experienced was universal.

The she-wolf should be half out of her mind, turned by force as she'd been, thrust into a ring to fight for her life, overcome by the sensations of a new body—by the sounds, scents, and emotions of others she would be experiencing nearly as strongly as her own until she learned how to tune them out.

But she was fighting. And not only was she fighting, she was fighting well, a feat that should have been just short of impossible given the circumstances and what her body must be going through.

It would be a shame for her to die.

But that choice had been taken out of their hands.

Hers was a fate worse than death. If Kisha or Ty didn't kill her, he'd have to.

The she-wolf was masking a limp as she paced,

trying to stay out of Kisha's reach. If not for Ty's reluctance in joining his pack wolf in attacking, the she-wolf wouldn't have had a chance. Two against one weren't fair odds, not even when she wasn't injured as she was.

He drank in the sight of her, fully aware how quickly wolves could kill, knowing the she-wolf would likely be dead by the time they managed to rescue their own.

A shame. A waste of a fighter spirit.

Without another look, he turned and led Lucian and Nolan back past the concession stand, ignoring the woman's offer of a drink.

No, he didn't want a drink. He wanted to murder everyone who supported this "sport." He didn't even look at the woman, certain that his eyes, which usually concealed the wolf violet decently well since his they were so dark, wouldn't fool anyone right then.

With Lucian and Nolan fast on his heels, he stalked across the marble tiled foyer, fervently hoping they'd have time to tear the place apart before they left. He didn't want to leave a stick standing. None of it. He wanted it all to burn.

Noticing how out of control his emotions were, he worked to rein them in. He wasn't beta of the Smoky Mountain Pack because he allowed his emotions to rule his decisions; any wolf could do that, and regularly did. Wolves were hotheaded and temperamental in the best of circumstances. They were also fiercely loyal and passionate about what they put their minds to.

Silver, he said, reaching through another limited pack link to include the wolves who'd gone the other way as well as Lucian and Nolan. *Where are you? What have you found?*

The only way for Silver to answer was through the pack link every one of their wolves could access, but it couldn't be helped.

This is for Quannah, Silver's voice arrived right away, sounding in his head as if the man with the silver flecks in his eyes, mixing with the violet, were standing next to him.

We're below ground. We found a bunch of cells. Lots of wolves have been here. We scent hundreds of them.

And Moore? Have you found him? Quannah asked so only the wolves at the Pound could hear.

A pause. *We have.*

Then that's enough. Quannah hurried to tell Silver and the others. If Silver hadn't told him the fate of their wolf, that could only mean one thing. He was dead, and Silver didn't want to tell the whole pack like this, especially as it wasn't his place.

Quannah would tell their alpha, and Corin would share the news with the pack.

Kisha and Ty are inside the arena fighting a she-wolf who's just been turned. There are a set of double doors and also a single door leading into the arena. Meet us on the other side of them. It's two against one. The she-wolf won't last long. When they bring Ty and Kisha back out, we'll take them.

They'd already crossed the foyer and were taking the turn back down the way they'd come.

And, Silver ... we'll want to take Moore's body with us.

Silver didn't answer. He wouldn't, not when everyone in the pack would hear his response.

Taking the hallway in the direction Silver, Webb, and Dax had gone, Quannah's step hitched.

The announcer's words came back to him.

Only one wolf was to remain standing at the end of the fight.

Neither of their wolves would hurt each other.

What would the mystery patron behind the Pound do when he realized the pack wolves wouldn't kill each other?

He broke into a nearly silent run, Lucian and Nolan right behind him.

CHAPTER NINE

QUANNAH

ONE LONG HALLWAY led into another, and then another, until they finally encountered a closed door that led to a set of stairs. The deeper they descended into the bowels of the Pound, the darker and danker the setting became. By the time Quannah, Lucian, and Nolan reached the arena level, the niceties of the foyer were long gone.

"Holy hell, man," Nolan whispered on a horrified gasp before catching himself and offering Quannah a grimace by way of silent apology.

But Quannah didn't blame him. He was thinking far worse and had barely managed to keep his own outrage quiet.

Dozens of cells lined the hallway that led to the arena, and just as Silver had, Quannah scented hundreds of wolves, most of them probably long dead.

He gritted his teeth against the curses that rushed forward to tumble from his own lips.

The smells marring the cells were foul, as if the wolves contained within hadn't had a choice but to urinate and defecate within them. The cells to the other side of the staircase were lined with regular steel bars, though thick ones.

But Quannah could smell the silver content. The bars of the cells closest to the doors that led to the arena contained enough silver to fry a wolf's skin on contact, shifters and werewolves alike.

He scented Ty, Kisha, and Moore within the depths of these cells. Ty's signature melded with the smell of silver, suggesting the wolf had been burned by it.

Beside him, Lucian breathed too heavily, like a bull preparing to charge, as Silver, Webb, and Dax stepped out from a deep shadow that had kept them out of sight.

When Quannah reached them, he noticed a pile of bodies stacked behind them, concealed by darkness. Three men. Guards, surely.

There was hardly any light down here. Unlit, bare bulbs hung from the ceiling. Dim yellow bulbs spaced every twenty feet along one wall were the only illumination. But for a wolf, it was more than any of them needed.

Silver, Webb, and Dax had only knocked out the three guards. That was the way of the Smoky Mountain Pack. They didn't kill unless they had to.

Right then, Quannah wanted to break their rules. From the fierce set to the other men's jaws, they were also regretting that the guards would wake in a while.

They'd had an idea of what they were walking into before arriving. They'd anticipated that a place that pitted wolves against each other in imitation of dog fights would be unpleasant.

But being here? Seeing, smelling, and feeling what happened here?

It was so much worse.

Where's Moore? Quannah asked using a limited pack link.

Dax pointed to a cell beside them. Nothing moved within, but Quannah made out an unmoving lump. One of their wolves, dead.

Lucian and Nolan growled softly. Moore had been like a brother to them, to all of them.

The door to the cell hung ajar as it did for most of the other empty cells, but this lock held a key, as if even dead, the Pound had held the wolf captive, and Silver, Webb, and Dax had found and used the key.

He goes with us, Quannah said, though it was

unnecessary. The flared nostrils, the eyes so angry they gleamed purple in the dim light, the twitching jaws and clenched fists all of them sported. None of them would leave Moore behind.

He had to keep his cool, so Quannah forced himself to look away from the dead body of his friend.

I thought we could wait to grab Ty and Kisha until they finished the fight and were brought back here, but the fight will have only *one winner*.

There was no need to say more. The others understood.

We have to grab them now, before they realize that Kisha and Ty won't kill each other.

Obviously, depraved individuals ran the Pound. Would they kill Kisha or Ty themselves if the wolves wouldn't obey? Probably.

They'd have to give their audience what it wanted, and right then the men and women lining the stands were clamoring for a bloody end. Their shouts sliced through the doors that led to the arena. They'd begun stomping their feet against the metal of the bleachers, and the rhythmic beat was speeding up, reaching for a crescendo.

Quannah breathed in, feeling the weight of the safety of the five men with him. He wished they could wait and take their wolves back here so as to minimize their risk.

But if they waited, they risked Ty and Kisha, and one dead pack wolf was already one too many.

Looking at Silver, Webb, and Dax, Quannah asked: *Have you found an exit down here?*

The men nodded, and Silver pointed forward, then left. The way out was down this hall, somewhere at the end of a left turn.

It didn't matter where the exit delivered them. Flynn and the other wolves would be close enough. They'd make it out of there. The Pound didn't look like it was expecting trouble.

Webb, Dax, Quannah said. *When I give the signal, you pull open the doors and you hold them open. When we come back through, you lock them again, with that bar too.*

Both fit, muscled men with brown hair, they nodded.

Quannah looked at Silver, Lucian, and Nolan. *As soon as those doors open, Kisha and Ty should run out. Ty is injured, but it doesn't look too bad. He's still moving well enough. If we open those doors and things have changed, our job is to pick them up if we have to and get them out.*

He turned toward Webb and Dax again. *You two carry Moore.*

He wanted to wait, to take a chance that Ty and Kisha might end up back here after all. Exposing themselves in the arena was far from ideal. But there wasn't time to wait, not when death could arrive so swiftly.

Quannah cracked his neck, the sound of it drowned out by the screams, stomping, and the loud speaker. Beneath it all, there were growls, snarls, and the tearing of flesh that couldn't be confused with anything else.

If we need to fight, we don't risk any wolves. Kill if you have to.

A wicked smile spread across Silver's face.

Move fast. Let's get our wolves and get the hell out of here. Once everyone's safe, we can figure out what to do about this place. I'll talk to Corin.

Which just meant that Quannah was going to try to convince Corin to raze the place to the ground. It probably wouldn't take that much convincing. Corin was measured, as any good alpha should be. But when something was wrong, he didn't hesitate to make it right.

Lucian stepped forward and cupped his hands in front of his chest in imitation of breasts. It wasn't a lewd gesture. He was asking what their beta wanted them to do with the she-wolf.

The she-wolf will be dead by now. Leave her.

The command slid through Quannah like poison.

But the she-wolf wasn't one of theirs. Her fate was out of his hands.

Zasha

Zasha's front leg was in bad shape; she was having trouble putting weight on it, let alone walking on it. For a while, the adrenaline rushing through her body masked the extent of the injury. Even if the announcer hadn't laid out the stakes, she'd have known. The only way she was getting out of this ring was if she killed at least one of the other wolves, maybe both of them.

It didn't matter how much she didn't want to hurt them. She wouldn't just lie down and die. She couldn't. Her father had sacrificed too much to give her a life.

And Black Rack would kill her if Zasha gave her the chance. She wasn't as certain about Wild Killer, but he wouldn't have a choice, not if he wanted to survive himself. No signs remained of his earlier resignation and acceptance of his death.

Zasha suspected that the bone of her front leg—

she had little idea about terms for the anatomy of a wolf—what would have been the tibia in a human, was broken. But it wasn't shattered, allowing her to force weight onto it.

The muscle was shredded, but she didn't think any tendons or ligaments had snapped, or she imagined her leg would buckle.

The attack could have been worse; if it had, she'd be dead by now.

Despite Wild Killer's interference, Black Rack wasn't holding back. Zasha had managed to pierce the other wolf's leg, but hadn't caused enough harm to impede Black Rack's sharp, predatory movements. The wolf was about to pounce again. The violet, pointed gleam of her eyes broadcast her intentions.

Zasha pushed away the sensation of her flesh hanging off her leg, refused to look down to examine the extent of the damage, and pushed away the cheering and jeering of the audience. She even managed to ignore the announcer, the constant of his voice fading into the din.

There was only her and two wolves pitted against her.

There was only life or death. Kill or be killed.

Black Rack swiped a paw at her, claws extended, and Zasha barely managed to jump out of the way in time.

Dammit, she had to focus more. The pain, combined with whatever dark magic ran through her, was making her mind foggy. This body, so foreign to her own, felt sluggish. She'd given thousands of hours of her life to preparing to defend herself, and now ... this. She'd never prepared for *this*.

Black Rack swiped another paw at her, and this time Zasha feinted out of the way, slower to swing back than she'd like, but still managed to thrust a paw forward and slice across Black Rack's side.

Zasha's injured leg buckled under the extra weight, and she fell awkwardly to her belly.

Black Rack squealed, but didn't fall. The cuts weren't deep enough.

She was already turning to come at Zasha again. Zasha forced herself to her feet. Her front leg wobbled and threatened to crumple again, but finally held. She bared her teeth and snarled at Black Rack.

The other wolf charged at her, and again Wild Killer slammed into her to stop her.

That was the second time he'd done that, and Zasha's sides heaved as she used the moment he'd bought her to recover.

Black Rack slammed back into him, hitting the raw flesh on his hindquarter. He stumbled, and Black Rack charged across the short distance separating her from Zasha.

This was it, Zasha thought. Her last chance. Black Rack was all swift animal efficiency. Zasha was broken in more ways than one. She feinted left to throw off the other wolf, but Black Rack anticipated her movement and landed her open jaw beneath Zasha's throat, chomping at the flesh on her chest, between her shoulders.

Black Rack's jaws clamped down, slicing through muscle.

Before she could inflict more damage, Zasha brought her own jaws down on top of the other wolf's head, sliding them downward until a canine tooth pierced the wolf's eyeball.

Black Rack grunted in pain and pulled back, taking a chunk of Zasha's chest with her.

Before Zasha collapsed, she lunged toward Black Rack again, ignoring the signs that her front leg was about to give out, and bit the wolf's hind leg.

She was about to thrash her head to either side to inflict maximum damage, when Wild Killer chomped on her tail—and didn't let go.

Zasha felt his teeth slice through the flesh beneath the fur…

Then a thud resonated above the din of the crowd and announcer.

They all froze, even Black Rack, who didn't take her gaze off her. Blood trailed down from one eye and into her chocolate brown fur. If she'd been angry before, she was seething with fury now.

Wild Killer whined in that way he had earlier, when he'd attempted to communicate with her. She didn't understand him now either, but Black Rack did.

She whipped her head around to look behind them and stilled.

Another thud, and Zasha risked looking behind them too.

She stared, and Wild Killer released her tail.

There, in the open doorway of the double doors, stood six men, fierce predators despite their human forms. They weren't human. Their eyes all glowed violet to differing degrees. Were they here to kill her too? If so, she was done for. There was nowhere she could go to avoid them. No way could she fight them off.

The man at the front stared at her with dark eyes threaded through with violet, set in a fierce face with angles so sharp they could cut. He was the one to be afraid of—if Zasha believed in being afraid. But she owed her father more than that. She owed herself more than that. Whatever happened, whatever came, she'd die fighting. She'd give everything she had to her survival.

She forced her body to cooperate and turned to

face them, only to see Black Rack running toward them, a slight limp hitching her stride.

With a whimper at her, Wild Killer took off after her.

CHAPTER TEN

QUANNAH

QUANNAH STARED AT THE SHE-WOLF. Not only was she alive, but she'd obviously hurt Kisha.

That shouldn't have been possible. Kisha was trained to fight. The dog-fight ring might be new to her, but that shouldn't change anything.

Kisha and Ty were running toward them—well, limping.

The people in the stands were momentarily stunned into silence. Even the announcer stopped speaking while everyone registered the cause of the interruption.

The silence didn't last long. The audience erupted into cries of alarm and discontent. If they'd been clamoring for blood before, they were screaming for it now.

The announcer called for security, and immediately the guards who lined the upper levels of the arena started moving. Had they been Smoky Mountain Pack wolves, Corin would have kicked them out. Their reaction time was deplorable; they'd frozen with their shock along with everyone else.

Quannah would take whatever advantages they could get.

"Come on, hurry," he called to Kisha and Ty, even though the wolves would reach them in seconds.

But Quannah had noticed a man in a VIP box stand with a cell phone to his ear. The man stared back at him, his eyes lighting up with a dark scarlet glow that betrayed him as something other than human.

Something that wasn't afraid of the wolves.

The man studied Quannah while the two bimbos with him cowered, cast a quick glance at the man, then at each other, before scurrying through a door behind them.

As Kisha and Ty reached their pack and barreled through the open doors between the men, the VIP man snapped his phone shut—a burner phone probably—and narrowed his eyes at Quannah, until they were threats all on their own.

The wolf waggled his jaw, not even hearing the

announcer's continued shouts for someone to stop the thieves.

The VIP man pointed at his eyes with two fingers, then at Quannah.

"Yeah, yeah," Quannah said, though the man wouldn't hear him. "I've got my eyes on you too, you fucking bastard. And I'm coming for you."

Catching sight of three guards at the bottom of the stands, struggling to unlock a gate in the chain-link fencing, Quannah turned and walked back through the open double doors, smiling wickedly. The guards' own attempts to keep their prisoners in would keep them from interfering in time.

Lucian, Nolan, and Silver followed him through the doors, and Webb and Dax yanked them shut, locking them before throwing the steel bar in place, making sure no guards were coming through this way—at least not easily.

Quannah stalked quickly down the hallway, grateful to be free of the blaring spotlights, when he heard the whining.

He stopped and turned, searching out Ty, who hadn't moved from next to the doors.

Webb and Dax, each carrying one end of Moore's body, raced past Ty. Kisha was up front, clearly ready to get the hell out of there.

"Come on, Ty," Quannah ordered.

But Ty, who'd known Quannah his entire life and never disobeyed a direct order from anyone higher in the pack hierarchy, didn't budge. He shook his head, then gestured behind him, through the doors.

"We've got to go now," Quannah said. "We'll make them pay later. We're getting you out."

Ty shook his head again, gesturing through the doors once more.

"Now, Ty."

But Ty turned, training his eyes on the doors behind him.

Quannah thought he understood. "We have to leave the she-wolf. She'll die anyway."

Ty shook his head yet another time, confirming that Quannah correctly guessed what he meant. Then he whined loudly, bobbing his head in the direction of the arena, making the other wolves up ahead pause and turn toward them.

Quannah growled. "There's no time for this. We're leaving right now, before their guards reach us."

And guards were coming their way. Every single one of them could hear the stomping footfalls as the sentries thumped down the staircases above them.

It wouldn't be long now.

Ty turned back around but didn't advance. He stared at Quannah with steady, stubborn eyes.

Quannah could spend all day arguing with Ty, but he knew the wolf well enough to understand. He'd allow the rest of them to leave him behind before abandoning the she-wolf.

"Dammit," Quannah said on a thick growl, already moving back toward the double doors.

He called orders behind him as he moved the bar out of place: "Webb, Dax, you get Moore out. Find Flynn. Lucian, Nolan, Silver, you're with me."

He didn't bother telling Ty anything; the wolf wasn't going anywhere without the she-wolf.

"She's probably already dead anyway," Quannah muttered, unlocking the deadbolts.

Flynn, he said only to the gamma. *We might be running into some trouble. Send the wolves in through the bottom exit into the cells. It's somewhere around the back. You stay out.*

Flynn received his message and understood exactly what Quannah didn't say. Flynn was to remain outside because Quannah might not make it out.

"Hurry," Flynn told the wolves with him. "They need help in there. Through the back bottom entrance into the cell area."

Before he'd even finished speaking, the remaining wolves were sprinting across the torn asphalt of the parking lot, around the building. To find the other members of their pack, they'd scent them once they got inside.

Flynn stared at the large industrial structure, willing every wolf to come back out of it. Its footprint covered most of a city block. And above ground it was several stories tall.

While Flynn waited, Quannah, Lucian, Nolan, Silver, and Ty swarmed into the arena.

Kisha didn't, waiting by the doors, flicking her gaze between the arena and the hallway containing the cells. The footfalls from above were closer.

She growled out her frustration, swearing to herself that she'd kick Ty's ass until he couldn't walk for a week for pulling this shit. Who cared about the she-wolf? She was going to die anyway.

Inside the arena, the she-wolf was facing off with the three guards who'd entered through the silver-lined fence. Several others were running across the stands down toward her, the announcer calling for her blood.

Quannah couldn't believe it. Not only was the she-wolf still standing, she was fighting.

Deep, crimson cuts already trailed down her chest, marring that odd-colored fur and dripping into the dirt beneath her paws. Her foreleg was a mess. Her chest was a bloody hole that heaved from exertion, and yet she bared her teeth at the men who drew clubs and electrified prods from their belts. Their prods were longer than the average tool used with stock animals. At least a foot and a half longer, they were designed to keep them away from wicked sharp teeth and claws.

She snarled loudly enough to be heard above the audience, most of which had rushed down the stands to lean into the railing that gave them a direct view into the arena beneath them.

When they entered the ring, Quannah's men hung back, waiting for his instruction. "She comes with us," he told them as Ty howled.

She turned, flicked her eyes from Ty, to him, to the three men running toward her, then back to the guards extending hot sticks and clubs toward her. Electricity crackled, slicing through the continuous shouts from above and across the sound system, and the she-wolf jumped back.

Her front leg buckled, but she was up and back on it in a heartbeat.

The blue electricity of another prod arced toward her. She dodged, whipped a look up at the VIP box, then turned and ran, glancing continuously behind her at the sentries who charged after her.

She passed Silver, Lucian, and Nolan, and limped toward the open doors. Kisha yipped from inside, and Quannah and Ty ran back through the opening.

Five muscled guards were charging toward Kisha, who faced them, her head lowered, a ferocious growl announcing her intentions. Hurt or not, Kisha would rip them to shreds if given the chance. They extended cattle prods toward her, the cowards.

"I wouldn't do that if I were you," Quannah said.

Ty shored up next to him, baring teeth.

"Oh yeah, and why shouldn't we?" asked the guard in front, his tone cocky. Wearing the same plain gray uniform the rest of them wore, he was six-foot-three and largely muscle. Even so, he wasn't as fast or as strong as a wolf, especially not one who hadn't been injured.

With the kind of ease of a man who only said what he meant, and could back up his threats, Quannah said: "Because I will make you pay if you hurt any of my wolves."

You guys good? he asked Silver, Lucian, and Nolan.

We got it, Nolan said, using the pack bond.

The entire Smoky Mountain Pack would probably be questioning what the hell was going on after all the partial, cryptic messages. Corin would definitely be wondering how things were going, but the alpha would know not to ask questions when they were in the middle of a mission. He was in another state on pack business, so there was nothing he could do to help them anyway.

The muscled sentry in the front didn't heed Quannah's warning, extending his prod toward Kisha. She jumped out of the way, lunging at his leg, but her depth perception was off thanks to her injured eye, and her jaws skimmed the loose hem of his pants.

Another guard lunged forward with his prod as if he were fencing, and slammed the crackling point of it into her face.

She howled and fell back, blood streaming down her face.

Ty whipped past Quannah.

"Halt," the beta snapped.

Ty stopped mid-attack, and instead moved to hover protectively over Kisha, snarling at the guards.

Quannah charged the muscled guard, sliding out of reach of his extending prod before ramming a hand into his elbow. The bone broke with a crunch, and the man fell to his knees with a cry. Quannah kicked the prod down the hallway, and stepped toward the next security guards.

Two of them rushed toward him, prods straight

out in front, electricity crackling. Quannah jumped out of the way to side-kick one prod, making sure to hit it with the rubber sole of his boot, grateful he'd chosen to wear the thick-soled boots instead of the moccasins that were his go-to. But everything about Flaming Arrow was nasty, and he hadn't wanted to soil his moccasins.

The prod flipped out of the guard's hand while the second one thrust toward him, and the other two guards circled.

Quannah danced out of the way, then rounded a man, and again broke an elbow. It was the most efficient way to disarm them and make sure they wouldn't be effective fighters when they got back up.

A prod dropped to the bare concrete floor with a loud clatter, and Quannah knocked it away. Then he kicked the first man in the chin, snapping his head back. He fell flat to the floor.

Quannah was going to do the same to the guard with the broken elbow, but the other two guards had reached him, and the first muscled man was standing up.

"Back up," he told Ty and Kisha, and he brought up his fists, bouncing on the toes of his heavy boots.

Guards charged him, a third back on his feet, holding his elbow, moving awkwardly behind them. Quannah kicked one in the center of the chest, making him stagger. Before he came at him again, Quannah dodged the punch another guard threw, and slammed the edge of his hand into his neck. The man choked out a strangled *umph*.

Quannah dodged another club, but it glanced off the back of his shoulder.

He spun, grabbed the rod, and whipped it hard, yanking the man's arm with it. When he had the guard off balance, he dropped his hold, punched him square in the diaphragm in a quick one-two-three, then delivered a powerful hook to the side of the jaw.

It was a lethal strike. He felt the man's neck snap with the force of his blow.

Ty growled sharply, and Quannah roved his attention around the circle of sentries. One of them was reaching for a large gun. He also noticed Flynn's wolves rounding the corner and running up the hallway.

Quannah deflected the hits of the other guards with quick jabs that knocked them off balance, moving for the guy with the gun. The guard was quick to train it on him. Behind him, two of the wolves reached for the discarded weapon, and zinged him with more electricity than the human body was designed to withstand. Pointed at Quannah, the guard with the gun jerked as the prods rammed into him, and the shot that was meant for the beta zoomed down toward Ty.

Quannah jumped into the path of the bullet.

It sliced through him with the firepower of a Dirty Harry hand cannon, knocking him to the floor. His head thunked against the hard concrete.

CHAPTER ELEVEN

ZASHA

ZASHA WATCHED the man with the dark hair and eyes enter the hallway, leaving the guards out in the arena to the three men who'd come to her rescue.

She'd grown up around fighters. Her father and uncles, when in their prime, had been bulldozers in the ring and cage. Though their bodies were all different, they were uniformly effective. The strength behind their punches and kicks was all but legendary.

But this man ... he moved with an elegant lethality she hadn't often witnessed in the ring, and never in a man his size. He was tall, his body lined with long, lean muscle. But he moved with the grace of a man half his size, light on his feet, striking with the speed of a viper.

With the threat behind her under control, and no

way out until the guards in front of them were dealt with, she had nothing to do but watch.

Five guards charged him, but he reacted and struck faster than any of them could coordinate an attack. Even with their weapons, they were no match for him. Bones snapped, and the guards crumpled to the floor, all but neutralized after a single blow.

Enraptured by the grace and strength of his movements, she welcomed the distraction from her mounting pain. Now that she wasn't under direct attack, her body was broadcasting the extent of her injuries. Like a loud foghorn, she wouldn't be able to ignore it for long.

Behind her, the three men bolted through the doors and hurried to shut them again. She was turned, watching them throw the bolts and drop the steel bar into the brackets designed for it, when the gunshot rang out.

At first, she thought she was hearing an echo—it must have been the bar clanging against the bracket. If not for the open mouths and wide eyes of the three men who'd come to her rescue, she might have believed that's all it was.

They rocketed past her, jostling her as they tore up the hallway.

When she faced Dark Eyes again, she discovered him on the ground, working to push up onto his hands. Wild Killer, Black Rack, and every other man down there charged the guards in a blast of chaos. They swarmed them, and those sentries who'd been standing went down hard.

The guard with the gun aimed at one of the other men. Another of them grabbed the sentry's arm, a second wrestled the weapon out of his hand, and a third picked it up.

That man pointed it at the guard's forehead and without any hesitation pulled the trigger. The gunshot echoed through the hallway, bouncing into the empty cells, leaving Zasha's sensitive wolf ears ringing.

Then they all started shouting, overpowering the commotion leaching through the closed doors and the announcer's increasingly panicked calls for security to keep the wolves from escaping.

She had no doubt Boss Man would try to make them all pay for their escape.

She didn't care. She just wanted to leave this place.

"Silver bullet," Dark Eyes uttered, and several of her rescuers swarmed in to help him up, supporting most of his weight as he wrapped an arm around a man's shoulders on either side.

"Make sure we have everyone," he said, allowing the others to help him out.

The man with the quick trigger finger continued to cover the four guards who lived, though none of them looked like they were considering attack at that point. Butts on the floor, they stared at the wolves as they retreated, cradling their various injuries.

When everyone else was down the hallway, taking a left out of there, Trigger Finger gestured at her with his head, his eyes never leaving the sight of the gun. "Come on, she-wolf. After all the trouble you caused, we're not leaving you behind."

She hadn't asked for anyone to save her, but that was an argument for another time—when she had a human mouth again and they were far from here.

Without a sound, she followed the others, her entire body aching with every step she took. By the time she reached the open door at the end of a long line of dark cells that reeked of desperation and resignation, she wasn't sure she could take another step on her leg, but somehow she made it out the doorway and into the stark sunlight that made her eyes hurt. Numb, she vaguely registered footsteps behind her and the shutting of the door with a loud, final clang.

One step after another, she followed the line of men and wolves as they jumped into cars. A man ran out of the driver's side of one of the cars to help Black Rack inside, and when it was her turn to get into the back of a van, the man with the gun tucked it into his waistband and lifted her inside with a soft grunt.

When the doors shut behind them, blocking out the bright sunshine, the van took off in a squeal of tires. She lost her footing and flew across the bare, metal floor of the vehicle, her paws sliding. With a thud that knocked the breath from her, she slammed into the man with the dark eyes, who lay on the floor, making him hiss.

"Watch yourself," snapped a man who pressed a cloth against Dark Eyes' bullet wound in a compress.

She might have apologized if she'd been a woman —but maybe not. It wasn't like she'd done it on purpose, and she didn't appreciate his tone. After all, she was injured too.

Dark Eyes had a bullet wound. She was torn to shreds all over.

The men on either side of Dark Eyes leaned over him, deep in discussion, ignoring her now.

"We need to get this silver out," one said.

"Not while we're moving like this. We could hurt him more."

"Us slicing him open won't hurt him worse than the silver. It's poisoning him."

The van hit a bump in the road and everyone caught air. Dark Eyes winced.

She growled at the van, at the shitty turns of her life, at everything.

"If we cut him open like this," the man on the right said, "we might cut something important. The bullet's too close to his heart."

"Which means the poisoning is even more dangerous."

"Look, I'm not arguing with you on that, Silver," the one on the right said. "But if we cut him open while Flynn is bouncing us around like a madman, things could get worse. Like *dead* worse. We have to wait. Flynn knows Quannah was shot with silver. He knows how bad it can get and how fast. We have to trust that he'll pull us over somewhere soon so that we can get this bullet out."

Silver huffed out his displeasure and pulled another clean cloth from a med kit, wrapping it for another compress. Dark Eyes—Quannah—had almost bled through the first cloth.

"Flynn had better stop soon," Silver said.

"Yeah, man, I know. Trust me, I know." Then the man glanced up toward the front of the van, as if through the sheet of steel he could urge the driver on faster. "The Pound wasn't ready for us. They won't pursue. We just need to get to someplace we can hide while we take care of Quannah."

But the way the man said it, he wasn't certain,

and her ears, more sensitive than ever before, registered the squealing tires and gunning motors trailing them.

They weren't alone.

Gideon

The way the Pound forced people to become monsters was deplorable—even he wouldn't argue otherwise. But today it had served its purpose.

Finally.

Gideon Slate could hardly contain his excitement as he pressed down on the accelerator of the 1950 Ford F1 pickup.

Five months of surveillance had thinly spread the ranks of the Protectors of Humanity, AKA the Society, in the northeast. And it had been his decision, which meant the success or failure of the mission was all on him. For months, when none of the monsters had shown up to rescue their own, he'd wondered if he'd made a bad call—if that mistake would cost him his place among the elite of the Society.

But the risk was paying off now.

The Pound might have trusted in the secretive nature of its location, but he'd known the wolves would eventually find it. In all the centuries the Society had watched the beasts, all across the world, their loyalty to each other had remained a constant. The monster wolves, much as their animal counterparts, moved in packs. They didn't abandon one of their own unless they had no other choice.

It had been how the Society had managed to trap so many of them over the years. The hunters relied on their foolish alliance to each other to trap them—to do their jobs.

And never had there been a more important calling than theirs.

It was the Society's duty to save humankind.

He'd seen firsthand how the wolves devastated entire villages, tearing their inhabitants to shreds as if they were nothing more than ragdolls. Children and the elderly discarded like trash.

Every member of the Society had witnessed similar carnage. It was part of the induction process into the Society, a necessary part of understanding why their missions were so vitally important. Why they had to put their duties above all else. Why so few of them had families of their own.

Without them, and the work they conducted in secret, humanity would surely perish. The beasts were never more than a few steps away from overrunning the world. They had no concern for humans, who, to them, were nothing more than meat, or victims to convert into monsters as foul as they.

The inconspicuous white van Gideon was following took a hard right turn. The other cars trailing it took lefts.

He didn't fall for the decoys.

Through his telescopic lens, he'd seen the shapeshifters load Quannah into the van. The beta of the Smoky Mountain Pack looked injured, which meant Gideon would follow that van to the ends of the Earth for the chance to take out a ruling member of one of the largest packs in North America.

Oh yes, Gideon knew all about the Smoky Mountain Pack—though it protected its secrets even more closely than the Pound. But he'd learned that any beast, just like any person, had its breaking point. With enough time, he could get anyone to talk. Long gone were the days when he'd been squeamish. The passing decades, and the horrors he'd witnessed at the hands of the half-humans, taught him that he didn't have the luxury of a conscience. That was for those who remained ignorant of the dangers that lurked in the shadows, just beyond their sight. He fought so that others wouldn't have to endure the nightmares he did, the images he'd never erase from his memories, keeping him up at night.

When the white van took the turn onto the highway, he gunned the Ford pickup, which was nothing like what it appeared to be on the surface—much like the men and women who turned into monsters. The irony pleased him.

While the Pound hadn't been properly prepared for the invasion, he'd had the old, outdated pickup outfitted for pursuit. On the outside, the truck appeared derelict, matching Flaming Arrow perfectly, as if the truck had been abandoned to the elements since the '50s. But he hadn't pinched pennies on the restoration job. The hood hid a big block engine that could outrun anything short of a racecar, and his tires were up to the job—with some mud purposefully slapped on them to disguise that the truck really was a lean, mean, monster-chasing machine.

Much like him. Gideon smiled.

This time, Quannah Shaw, who carried the pack surname that meant "wolf" to any lover of ancient languages, wasn't going to get away from him.

This victory was *his*.

The Society would never doubt his decisions again once he took down the beta of the Smoky Mountain Pack and every single wolf with him.

CHAPTER TWELVE

QUANNAH

QUANNAH HAD WATCHED wolves die of silver poisoning enough times to know how it was going to go if they didn't get this bullet out of him soon. Even then, there was no guarantee he'd recover. If too much silver leached into the bloodstream, and then to the rest of the system, recovery became impossible despite the advanced healing of the wolves. That preternatural healing only activated once the silver was removed, and if too much damage had been done by then, at times it was simply too little, too late.

If Flynn didn't stop soon so Silver could dig out the bullet, it was going to be the end of him. The compresses Webb kept switching out and pressing against his wound were doing nothing but keeping his blood from coating the floor of the van.

Unfortunately, they couldn't afford to stop

anytime soon. Obviously they'd been wrong in thinking they'd taken the Pound and its VIP man completely unawares. Someone was pursuing them. From the floor of the van, he couldn't see what kind of vehicle it was, but it was fast and on their tail. The van began to slow.

Immediately, Quannah reached for Flynn through a limited link. *Do* not *stop*, he ordered.

Only after Flynn accelerated again did he add: *They're too close to us. If you stop, they'll have everyone in the van. Keep going until we lose our tail.*

Quannah understood that would probably be too late for him. Weaker only than Corin, he was stronger than most of the pack wolves. But "stronger than most" didn't mean much when his opponent was silver.

Even so, he was prepared to pay the price for his command. As a beta, his duty was to protect the pack, not himself.

He easily identified the signs of silver poisoning as they swept through him. In his lifetime, he'd been stabbed by a silver blade, shot with a silver arrow, and sliced by a silver sword, all courtesy of the hunters. Over the years, he'd seen hundreds of wolves endure the same. Every passing moment was the ticking of the second hand that counted out what he had left of his life.

His heart was slowing. His veins were constricting to protect themselves from the flow of silver-laced blood wanting to rush through them. The silver was everywhere inside him, spreading to his organs. Eventually, his lungs would squeeze in an attempt to reject the invasion of poison. His muscles would constrict. Everything about him would instinctively try to expel the venom. If they removed the bullet in time, and he was able to rest, keeping his body still to prevent pumping his blood and spreading the affliction, his body might have a chance to heal. The process would be slow and arduous, and his recovery not guaranteed until his body had fully expelled every speck of the silver. *I'm not going to be able to lose the truck tailing us in time*, Flynn's voice warned through the pack link, meaning that every one of their wolves was listening. *It's too fast. I can't shake it. We need to pull over. We can fight one truck off. It's just a pickup. There can't be but two or three people in there.*

When Quannah didn't answer right away, Flynn added: *We can call the other cars back to help us. We'll take out the truck, get the silver bullet out fast, and then keep moving. But, Quannah, we have to get the silver out. It's been too long.*

Quannah watched Silver and Webb share a look across his prone body, but it wasn't necessary to understand that what Flynn was doing was double-edged. Not only was the gamma combating every potential argument, but he'd just broadcast to their alpha that Quannah had been shot with silver and his commands had left the bullet in too long already.

Quannah didn't bother addressing Flynn just yet. He reached for that invisible thread, which he could feel whenever he focused on it, the one that connected him, and him alone, to their pack's alpha.

If Flynn stops now, everyone else will be at risk. The Pound is chasing us. We got Kisha and Ty out, and everyone else is safe. Moore was already dead when we got there.

It felt wrong to speak of Moore's death so casually when the man had been so fun-loving and full of life. But Quannah wouldn't risk anyone else.

If we stop now, we can't be sure we won't lose another wolf. For all we know, the truck behind us is loaded with a silver arsenal. It's not a risk I'm willing to take.

Despite the fact that Corin was in another state, he'd be able to hear his beta. The fact that he didn't answer right away meant he was deciding.

Quannah waited, struggling to breathe through all the sensations of his body resisting the silver while slowing down. Already, it was more difficult to suck in a breath. His vision had grown slightly blurry, and it wasn't because he'd banged his head on the concrete.

Flynn, Corin's voice finally arrived, sharp despite the delay. *Pull over now. Every pack wolf is to offer support while the bullet gets removed.*

Quannah tried to sigh, but his lungs clenched uncomfortably inside his chest.

Flynn all but slammed on the brakes, slowing abruptly, the van bouncing as he pulled them over on a rough shoulder. Every car filled with wolves would be doing U-turns at Corin's order and rushing their way.

Corin's voice filled Quannah's head. *I'm not losing you.* This time the words were only for him. *Get your ass home.*

Before the van had even come to a full stop, Silver was tearing through the med kit while Webb ripped Quannah's shirt in half.

Zasha

Zasha huddled into the corner of the van nearest the doors. Now that the adrenaline had begun to seep from her within the illusion of safety provided by the vehicle, she could barely move. The men tending to Quannah were a whirl of frantic intervention, and she didn't want them to knock into her. Her battered body couldn't take another hit.

When the driver of the van pulled over, she wished she could shout out that somebody was following them. But she was still a wolf who couldn't talk, a limitation that definitely wasn't helping her situation.

She was left hoping the vehicle behind them was friendly. Why else would they pull over?

Even so, she wasn't convinced. Of all the men in the van with her, she clearly understood the least. She stared up at them from over her torn leg.

The man named Silver had a scalpel and tongs in one hand while he emptied several vials of liquid from the med kit and stuffed these into his front shirt pocket.

When the sound of both front doors wrenching open reached their ears, Webb stared at Silver.

"Flynn and Cassie are out."

Silver nodded, but didn't stop moving. "If it sounds like they need you, you go. I can handle this without you, so long as you buy me time."

"I'm going now," the man with the gun said. "I'll give you all the cover I can."

Without another word, Trigger Finger pulled the handle on the inside of the doors, peeked through the crack between the two, jumped outside, and slammed the doors shut behind him.

The instant the van stopped shaking from the impact of the doors closing, Silver pulled the top off one of the vials with his teeth and told the man across from him: "Compress off." Then he poured the entirety of the vial's contents over the open wound visible on Quannah's bare chest, and tossed the empty glass container to the side without looking.

Quannah gritted his teeth, but didn't complain as the liquid hissed and sizzled, sounding like it was frying his flesh.

Silver tugged the top off a second vial, again with his teeth, and poured some of the liquid over the scalpel and forceps. Then he pushed the lid back in, and tossed it with his teeth back into his pocket. The vial landed atop the others with a clink.

Gunshots and shouts rang outside the van, making Zasha startle. But she didn't remove her attention from Dark Eyes.

Silver sliced open the corners of the wound with sharp, quick cuts of the scalpel, while telling his patient: "The bullet didn't exit. Hang tight."

The angular lines of Dark Eyes' face contorted while Silver carved, then slid the tongs into the wound, stretching it open.

Quannah's eyes watered, but he held perfectly

still. Silver's hand didn't so much as tremble as a bullet zinged the van, piercing a hole through the door and into the wall opposite Zasha.

Webb ducked. "Damn, that was close."

Sunlight now pierced the dim interior of the van through the bullet's entry and exit points.

Zasha hunched further into herself as the gunshots rained mere feet away from them.

Silver grimaced as he dug the tongs deeper into the wound.

Quannah blinked rapidly to ward off the pain.

"Fuck ... I've almost got it." Silver strained as he tried to get a firm hold on the bullet. The metal tongs kept sliding across the silver, slippery with all the blood. "Webb, I need you to keep the wound open. Got it?"

Webb nodded and grabbed the forceps from him, holding them open exactly as he had.

Silver lowered his face closer to the gaping hole in Quannah's chest and cut some more of the flesh back deep inside the wound.

Zasha winced with empathy. That had to hurt like a bitch.

But Quannah didn't so much as move a muscle in complaint.

Silver took control of the tongs again, and Webb dropped his hand, looking from what Silver was doing to the back doors of the van. It had grown suspiciously quiet out there.

Silver kept the scalpel inside Quannah's chest, pressing the flesh down and out of the way while he dug around some more with the forceps.

He hissed, yanked, and held up the tongs victoriously.

A single silver bullet, coated in bright red blood. It was larger than an average bullet, though Zasha didn't know what caliber it was.

Silver slid the scalpel out carefully and tossed it to the side of the van, along with the discarded vial.

"Got it. Let's go!" he yelled toward the doors, just as several gunning engines and squealing tires converged on their location.

Silver looked up at Webb, pulling the half empty vial back out of his pocket. "Go. I'm good now."

Webb didn't even respond. He rose to a crouch, squat-walked toward the doors, peeked out as Trigger Finger had, and slipped out. The doors clicked shut behind him as Silver poured the remaining contents of the vial over the now gaping wound in Quannah's chest.

The beta gritted his teeth, then chuckled dryly. "Never let anyone tell you that you lack a gentle touch."

"For you, the gentlest," Silver said around the lid

pressed between his lips, tossing the second vial and spitting out the top. "If I have anything to do with it, you'll live still, old man."

Then Silver pulled an empty vial from the med kit, uncorked it, dropped the bullet into it, sealed it, and put it back in the kit before tossing the tongs into the pile with the accumulating discards.

He slid a third vial from his pocket, uncapped it, brought his other hand under Quannah's head, and helped him drink its contents.

"Let's hope it's not too late for this to work," Silver said, then set his patient's head back down on a folded garment of some sort, patting him on the hand. "Don't give up on us, old man. We've got use for you yet."

"Shut up," Quannah grumbled. "I'm no older than you."

Silver smiled. "Could've fooled me the way you're just lying there ready to die, telling Flynn to keep driving till the poison took you too far."

"The needs of the pack come before the needs of a single wolf."

"Not when you're that wolf."

Quannah opened his mouth to protest. Silver shook his head. "Now shut it. You have to rest. Try not to move or speak. You're not out of the woods yet."

Quannah adjusted the shoulder closest to the wound, regretted the movement, then stilled and closed his eyes.

The sound of tires ripping up gravel slid into the back of the van. Rubber squealed against pavement as an engine revved, whipping past them.

Zasha heard whatever car had just raced past them shift through several gears before settling into fifth—too fast.

Then the doors to the van yanked open.

Zasha jumped, caught sight of several cars behind them, all with people getting into them.

Trigger Finger and Webb climbed back into the van, pulled the doors closed behind them, as the two front doors slammed shut.

Within seconds, they were taking off. What she couldn't tell was, were they in pursuit of whatever car had left them in the dust?

She received her answer soon enough. Flynn wasn't driving anywhere near fast enough to catch up with the car that had raced off.

She tried to get her muscles to relax again—because *damn* she hurt everywhere—when she noticed Silver's attention on her.

He slid over to her on his butt, she suspected so as not to risk tumbling onto her if the van should shake.

"I don't know if you can understand me," he said, looking into her eyes.

She nodded.

"Okay, good." He pulled out another two vials from his shirt pocket, the final ones. "We can't take the time to patch you up now, but this will disinfect your wounds. Two of them look pretty nasty."

Yeah, they felt pretty nasty.

"Why waste our supplies?" Trigger Finger said, and she tilted her head at him in the most ferocious glare she could manage.

He didn't even bother meeting it. "She's going to die anyway, and you have to make those special."

"Don't be a dick, Hayes," Silver told him.

Trigger Finger just shrugged. "It's not about being a dick. It's the truth."

Then Silver poured the contents of one of the vials over the gaping flesh of her foreleg, and Hayes' doomsday prediction fled her mind.

She panted, waiting for the sharp, stinging pain to pass. It didn't, and she wondered if she might pass out. The sensations clouding her mind were akin to those she resisted in the ring, working to prevent a knockout.

When he poured the liquid from the second vial over the open flesh of her chest without a moment's reprieve, she howled and blinked back the way her vision tried to cloud.

"Look at that," Silver commented to the others, not her. "She's a fighter. She looks like she's about to pass out."

Hell yeah she was a fighter. Through her ragged breaths, she willed herself to remain alert.

She wasn't safe yet. And she'd never be secure if anyone believed she was weak. Hadn't the Pound, with its Magic Man and Boss Man proven that?

CHAPTER THIRTEEN

ZASHA

THEY DROVE FOR SEVERAL HOURS, stopping only once to get gas. She'd had to pee most of the way, but she didn't get out of the van when they opened the back doors. She wasn't sure she could move. After Silver poured the liquid over the worst of her wounds, and the brutal sting finally faded, a welcome numbness settled across the open flesh. She didn't want to risk dislodging it. Besides, what if they left before she returned from doing her business? No one seemed overly concerned about her. Or what if she freaked out the other patrons of the gas station when they saw a wolf? The other wolves, Wild Killer and Black Rack, probably remained within the multiple vehicles...

She held her bladder, which meant that by the

time they arrived at their final destination, she really had to go.

Quannah hadn't moved once during their journey, and when the doors opened once more, two new men hopped up inside the van with a stretcher, the kind used with ambulances. Quannah remained so still while the new men, with the help of Silver and Webb, slid the gurney under him, that Zasha worried he might have died somewhere along the way.

She wasn't the only one to look at him with concern.

"Damn, he's in bad shape," one of the new guys said. "How long was that bullet in him?"

Silver frowned with a look at his patient. "Too long."

While Webb adjusted the straps on the cot, he said: "If Corin hadn't made Flynn stop, the stubborn bastard would've kept us going till he died."

Everyone, including Zasha, looked at Quannah. Those dark eyes closed, he didn't react. Long, black lashes lay against his cheeks, unmoving.

"It didn't help that the asshole who shot him used a .600 caliber," said Trigger Finger—Hayes.

"A .600?" another of the men asked. "What the hell? That's uncalled for."

"Don't worry," Hayes said, petting the shiny gun

tucked into his waistband. "The guy won't be pointing cannons at anybody else."

Silver's gaze slid to him. "You killed him?"

"Sure did." Hayes didn't blink while he held Silver's stare—until Silver finally nodded.

"Quannah did give us permission to kill if we had to," Webb said, hands on his thighs as he prepared to help lift their beta.

With a steely-eyed look at Silver, Hayes added: "Before you go giving me shit about whether or not I had to shoot the asshole, he'd already shot Quannah, and he was pointing the gun at the rest of us."

"The gun that you clearly took away from him."

Hayes continued to stare at him, unapologetic. "Those other guards were carrying weapons too. I shot the guy in the forehead. When he went down, the other guards decided to play nice. If I hadn't killed him, the others might've taken more of us down."

Silence circled the inside of the van, where it seemed to Zasha like all the men had forgotten she was there—huddled off to the side, out of the way.

Eventually, Webb nodded. "I'm glad you killed him. They were out for blood. And did you see where they kept our wolves?" He shook his head. "*Disgusting*. And to think Moore died there..."

"Moore ... died?" asked one of the new arrivals in a strangled voice.

Webb squat-walked over to the man, patting him on the back. "Shit, Jett. I'm sorry, man. I thought you knew."

Jett ran a hand through shabby dirty-blond hair, his shoulders sagging as he sat roughly on the large steel bumper as if his legs could no longer hold his weight.

"Waiting for Corin," Quannah announced in a rough rasp, making everyone but Jett swivel in his direction. "It's the alpha's place to tell, not mine."

"How'd he die?" Jett asked, staring off at a view Zasha couldn't yet see.

Despite the beta's comment, everyone waited for him to provide the information.

He started to speak, cleared his throat, and then continued. "Don't know yet. Could've been the conditions they kept them in, or an injury from a fight. The rumors were true. They pitted the wolves against each other like in a dog fight, or a cock fight. As if we're nothing but animals."

"It could've been one of the guards," Hayes said, outrage singeing his theory. If any of the sentries had been there, she suspected he wouldn't hesitate to shoot another one of them through the head.

Quannah shifted his shoulder with a grunt,

though he only moved it maybe an inch. "We'll find out what happened and give Moore the respect in death he was refused at the end of his life. Silver, you'll examine him."

It was half command, half question.

Silver sighed and ran a hand through hair nearly as black as the beta's, though his skin was much lighter.

"Yeah, of course I'll examine him. I just … really wish I didn't have to."

Jett sighed loudly, the sound hitching as his shoulders shook. Zasha couldn't make out his face, but she suspected he was working hard not to cry.

Quannah sighed too, carrying the weight of more lives than his own. "I also want you to take a look at Ty and Kisha. I think they might have been given a drug, street name Wolf Woofer. The guy Cassie found says the drug keeps them from shifting, slows their healing, and keeps them from accessing the pack link."

Everyone, even Jett, stared at Quannah, who suddenly looked exhausted, his face drawn, the hollows beneath his cheeks deeper, as if he'd lost ten pounds on the ride over.

"That's some crazy shit, man," Hayes said. "They all deserve to die."

None of the men disagreed.

"One thing at a time," Quannah finally said. "For now, Silver needs to take a look at all of us, including the she-wolf over there." As one, the men's attention landed on her. "Then we wait to see what Corin wants to do."

"And if that man from the Pound tracked us here?" Hayes asked.

"Then we show him what we think of being hunted like dogs, and we dispatch him where he belongs."

It was unclear where exactly that was, but Zasha didn't think it was anywhere fun.

"Come on, let's move," Quannah said, and Silver, Webb, Jett, and the other new guy lifted the gurney easily, gingerly lowering their beta from the van, and out of her sight.

Leaving her with Hayes, the one who thought her life wasn't worth wasting a tonic on.

He edged toward her, arms extended.

Had she had words, she would have told him where he could shove his intentions to lift her out of there. Given that she didn't, and she had no idea where they were, she didn't protest when he cradled her in his arms and carried her out of the van, with more gentleness than she thought him capable of.

Even so, she made sure he knew she wasn't pleased with the arrangement, narrowing her wolf eyes to slits, and pinning them on his face and its three-day-old scruff.

"Down, girl," he said over a chuckle, and she briefly considered peeing on him. It would serve him right.

But he was being careful not to grab her anywhere she was hurt, which was most places.

When she decided he wasn't going to drop her, she looked away from him and discovered herself in the most beautiful forest she'd ever seen. The trees were lush and tall, their leaves a verdant green. The sky was a crystalline blue, the clouds fluffy and white, and the sunshine warming as it peeked through tree canopies. The air was sweet and clean, and it felt amazing as it rustled through her fur. It whisked away the weight of the city. Flaming Arrow had been like an infectious disease she'd had to carry all her life.

Was this what her father had dreamed for her? The reason he kept insisting she leave the filthy city behind —and him? Had he known a place like this existed?

Hayes carried her up a porch and through a door.

Quannah, Black Rack, and Wild Killer were already on the other side of it.

THE ROOM WAS spacious and airy, with evenly-spaced windows that allowed in plenty of natural light, and were currently wide open. Views of trees occupied every pane, and raw wooden beams capped the high ceiling.

Zasha figured it wouldn't be a bad place to recover.

Clearly, the place was an infirmary of some sort. Unlike in human hospitals, like the one her father had checked into and never left, there was no scent of antiseptic masking other underlying foul smells. No, the large room with adjoining bathroom smelled more like what she imagined an apothecary of old might smell like. Herbs and spices scented the air, and a distilling station of some sort adorned a corner of the room, taking up most of it with its colored glass bottles, vials, and copper cauldron—yes, a cauldron.

The room also contained several dog beds large enough to accommodate wolves the size of Wild Killer, along with three human beds. Quannah already occupied one of them, and Wild Killer and Black Rack rested in two of the cushy animal beds.

Hayes laid her in another one of them before leaving the room without a word.

Immediately, she tensed, wondering where exactly she was, when she'd be able to get out of there, and how she could protect herself in a world obviously dominated by magic. The room even smelled like magic, if magic had a scent, and she suspected it did—like tangy copper, spicy herbs, and smoky sage.

She was in a strange place, with strange people—no, *creatures*, *monsters*—and she was in an even stranger body. For Zasha, there was nothing more uncomfortable than not being able to care for herself or understand what steps she could take to find her way back to her true self. To the body of a woman. To what remained of her family. They would be mourning her father; she had to be there with them.

But she couldn't even talk!

Silver, a woman apparently named Chenoa with long dark hair as thick as Quannah's, and a petite redhead named Roan, whose expressions shifted almost constantly in a fluid animation, tended to their beta.

From what Zasha gathered from listening to their conversation, along with their attempts to convince Quannah to convalesce in his own home where he'd be more comfortable, this wolf pack they were all a part of operated on a hierarchical system. A man named Corin was the alpha; next came Quannah who was their beta; and then Flynn, who was their gamma, the third in rank. After that, she had no idea how they determined station; it sounded like there were hundreds of wolves somewhere on the property. But no one had sidled up to offer her a condensed rundown of where she was or what any of it meant. There was no 101 tutorial on wolf shifters.

The beta was clearly their priority. Even Black Rack and Wild Killer, whose names were actually Kisha and Ty, were waiting to be tended to.

Silver, Chenoa, and Roan finished their ministrations of Quannah, which left him all fresh, clean, bare-chested, and bandage free. Silver said his wound would heal best in the open air. After a final suggestion that he might want to retreat to his home, and another growl from the beta saying he was staying here until he was sure Ty and Kisha were all right, Silver turned his attention to the three of them.

After a quick inspection of the other two wolves, he knelt next to Zasha, looking her over.

"I'll stitch you up as soon as I'm finished with Ty and Kish. But..." He shook his head, silver flecks seeming to swirl amid the violet of his eyes. "I honestly have no idea how you're still alive. Were you a wolf before arriving at the Pound?"

She shook her head vehemently, wanting to say, "Hell no, I wasn't. Those jerkwads made me this way." Instead, she only caused herself pain by jostling the open wound in her chest.

"So you were made a wolf ... by dark magic?" he

asked, and she noticed that everyone in the room, including Quannah, was paying attention.

Her eyes darted across everyone, then she nodded.

He whistled. "Then I don't get it." He turned to look at Quannah. "Do you? She should be out of her mind, drooling on herself by now."

"Maybe she just got turned," Quannah said.

"Hmm. Maybe." Silver faced her again. "How long ago were you turned? A month?"

She shook her head.

"Longer?"

No.

"Okay. A week?"

She shook her head again.

"Longer?"

No.

"A day?"

She nodded.

His eyes widened, and without another word he turned to look at Quannah another time.

"That can't be," Dark Eyes said.

Yeah, well, it is, she thought, wishing she could just say it.

"If that's the case," Dark Eyes continued—as if she would lie about something like that—"then there's something unusual going on."

No shit, Sherlock. She narrowed her wolf eyes at him, though it wasn't his fault Magic Man had made her a freak—a monster.

He noticed, but didn't react other than to stare back at her. "We'll figure her out. Let's see if she can change back first."

Her head jerked upward in surprise. So she *could* change back to human?

"That's right, she-wolf," Dark Eyes said. "If you've managed to survive the dark magic this long, maybe there's a chance that you can shift back to your human form, just like the rest of us do."

Hope.

That gave her *hope*.

"Heal up and we'll see what's possible," he added, but she already wanted to kiss him—or lick him, whatever. He'd given her the most important gift he could have; he'd given her reason to keep fighting.

She was used to battling impossible odds. She'd been the underdog her entire life. If anyone could do it, she could. Once she got stitched up, she'd start to heal. Then she'd see what she was capable of. They all would.

It wasn't much, but it was the start of a plan. It was more than she'd had in the desolation of her prison cell. At least they'd gotten her out of there.

Wherever they were now, this forest was a million times better than the smelly underground dungeons of the Pound.

Quannah looked at Ty and Kisha, careful not to move much.

"Guys, we're guessing you were drugged with something called Wolf Woofer that blocks your ability to shift, access the pack link, and heal fast. Does that sound right?"

Oh, they hadn't been in the van with them when Quannah mentioned the drug earlier.

The gray wolf and the chocolate-brown wolf nodded.

"Okay, then from what we understand, the only thing to do is wait until the drug works its way out of your system. Silver can probably give you something to speed that up, yeah?"

Silver walked toward the laboratory in the corner that looked like it belonged in a movie about wizards from a time long past. "I'll get on it right now. I'll do that; and Chenoa and Roan can stitch them and the she-wolf up."

So they'd recover together...

Now that Zasha had something to focus on, a goal, she sent all her energy toward healing. Her uncles and father had taught her more than fighting. They'd taught her that where her attention goes, her energy follows—that there is power within thoughts and intentions.

So she focused on seeing this body she was so unfamiliar with whole and strong, and all the while she listened to whatever conversations took place around her, trying to pick up on cues that might inform her where exactly she was and what was in store for her.

CHAPTER FOURTEEN

GIDEON

GIDEON WASN'T A SMILER, hadn't been for a long time. There was too much that went bump in the night—and the middle of the day—for him to find all that much to celebrate in life. He'd lost too many colleagues to the monsters, too many friends; he'd witnessed too many tragedies. It was impossible to forget how quickly people he cherished could be snatched away from him.

It was why he'd never allowed himself to fall in love, though Amalie Moreau had come close to stealing his heart despite his efforts to resist her charms. But she'd just been so damn charming. She'd been such a large presence that he'd found himself sucked into the current that led him always to her.

It had been that way for years, when they'd been new to the Society—or at least to active roles within it. Both born to families that had been part of the Society since its founding, they'd always known what their purpose in life would be. And even though they'd grown up well aware of how many monsters prowled the world, it was easier to ignore the weight of so much danger when they were young and fresh to combat.

After all these years, if he closed his eyes, he could still smell the scent of fresh forest and flowers that seemed to follow her wherever she went. He could still see the bright brown of her eyes that shifted color nearly every time he found himself staring into them. The way her lips, so bright and smooth, felt against his.

He hadn't seen her for twenty-some years, since that night in a small Northern French town when a run-in with some monsters hadn't gone as they'd planned. When they'd taken her from him and turned her right in front of him—or maybe they'd eaten her; he hadn't been able to tell. There'd been so much pain, so much blood. He'd never erase the sounds of the two wolves' gnashing teeth and snarls as they brought their faces to that bright, unmarred flesh.

The usually lovely Amalie, with her fresh, bright face and ever-present smile that illuminated her eyes, had screamed for longer than seemed possible, all the while holding his gaze across the small plaza, which the locals had abandoned at the first hint of trouble. The windows of the buildings lining the plaza had remained firmly shut, the shutters bolted closed. No eyes peeked out to witness the horrors occurring right outside their homes.

They knew of monsters in that town. They understood what they were capable of. They'd been the ones to call in the hunters and ask for their help. No one would come to their rescue.

Gideon and Amalie hadn't come alone. No, there'd been several of them. A team of new trainees, the mission was supposed to be easy, a great way to break them in. Their trainer had pronounced them ready, and when the villagers had contacted the hunters to tell them about the one lone, rogue werewolf, Gideon, Amalie, and the four others had jumped at the chance to prove themselves. Armed with sniper rifles chambered with silver bullets, their plan was simple. Watch the town until they spotted the wolf, shoot it on sight, and then leave town as victors, their first kill under their belts.

But when they'd arrived at the quaint village and positioned themselves strategically to spot the wolf before it saw them, everything that could have gone wrong did. Even though they'd taken precautions to mask their scents, rubbing on special oil that was supposed to make them smell like rotting compost and not like people, the monsters had turned the roles on them.

Gideon, Amalie, and the others had been the hunted in the end.

The villagers had been wrong. There wasn't just one wolf. There were several. And they'd had no trouble picking them off one by one as they'd positioned themselves separately upon the advice of their trainer to make sure at least one of them had a shot of the wolf.

When Gideon and Amalie heard the first of the screams and realized what was happening, they'd run toward each other to face this invisible threat together. In the dark of the night, they couldn't make out where their other teammates were. Either way, by then it didn't matter. Their screams were brief and shrill, the silence that followed heavy with the message of their fate.

When they'd come for Amalie, neither Gideon nor she had heard a thing before she was snatched off of his arm. One had held a gun, the other her with an iron hold. One moment she was there, pressed against his body, her warmth radiating into him, dispersing the cold chill of the night, steadying his racing heart, the very next she was gone, as if she'd never been there at all.

He'd swirled, searching for her, but all he'd caught was the rustling of leaves in the trees surrounding him—and in several directions, as if there were several wolves, all traveling different ways.

He'd hesitated for several seconds he didn't have to waste, then she screamed and he took off in a blind run toward the sound.

He tripped over a tree root or a rock, he didn't know, didn't care. He got back up, kept running, uncaring that branches raked him like the fingers of monsters snagging and whipping at his face.

He clutched his gun and ran like he'd never run before.

Then he finally saw her. Stretched out beneath two wolves. There was nothing he could do to save her. She realized it too. Her eyes, those deep, magical brown eyes, broadcast what she wanted him to do.

Tears streaming down his face, snot draining into his mouth, he brought the gun up toward her. He didn't aim at the wolves. There were fates far worse than death, and Amalie and he had spoken of this exact scenario. She didn't want to be turned into a monster any more than he did.

He might have only seconds before the wolves dragged her away, where they'd make her one of them. Already, there was no saving her; her blood ran freely from their mouths.

As they bent back over her, he held her eyes while his entire body shook. He was suddenly so cold in the night that hadn't seemed all that cold minutes before.

The wolves clamped their jaws around her arms and started to drag her away.

And Gideon took the shot.

He didn't have time to switch the silver out for a regular bullet.

So he'd shot her straight through with silver, ending her life. Ending her future torment.

He'd been raised with guns, with the mission. With a sense of duty. His shot had been a kill shot. Her screams had ended abruptly.

To protect the dead mass that his heart was rapidly becoming, he'd lied to himself. He'd never loved her at all. Love was one luxury hunters weren't allowed to have. He'd never forget it.

With effort, Gideon tore himself free of the memories. Thinking about Amalie and all that could have been never got him anywhere. He hadn't even been able to retrieve her body to give her a proper farewell.

He could also do without the doubts that had plagued him ever since then. Why had the monsters left him alive? Why hadn't they come for him just as they'd come for his teammates? He'd even waited around, giving them the chance to end him.

He gave the Ford pickup some gas, the engine revved in response, and the vehicle lunged forward. He still had another hour to drive before he reached the Society's chapterhouse beyond Flaming Arrow, because no one wanted to be any closer than necessary to the infested city and its filth. But the city of half a million people was a hub of supernatural activity. It was his job as head of the Flaming Arrow chapter of the Society to keep an eye on all of it.

The grin that tugged at his lips now felt awkward, as if his muscles had forgotten how to move that way. Regardless, it wasn't a friendly thing.

He'd trailed the beta back to the hub of the Smoky Mountain Pack. He'd just found the Holy Grail, the location of one of the largest and strongest packs in all of North America. He was definitely getting a promotion out of this. Maybe he'd finally be invited to join the higher-ups that met to decide what the Society did and where it placed its focus. After thirty-two years, every single one dedicated to the cause, he'd certainly earned his place among them.

The white unmarked van that contained the injured beta, and the cars following it, had practiced evasive measures—as usual. Members of the Society had been trying to pinpoint their location since they'd been made aware the pack existed. But they were always careful.

Even though he didn't think they'd spotted him again after he sped off since he'd stayed well out of sight, they'd still made multiple unnecessary turns, looping around each other. They'd taken a roundabout way back to the forest. If Gideon hadn't managed to tag them with a tracker, he would have never figured out where they'd disappeared.

His smile stretched.

They probably thought he'd raced off because he was outnumbered. But he didn't fear them, not anymore. He understood that any day he headed out in the name of the mission might be the day he died. Death didn't frighten him, Amalie's fate did. It was why he carried a potassium cyanide capsule with him everywhere he went. He even showered with it, housed in a waterproof necklace around his neck.

No, he hadn't driven off because they'd bared their teeth. He'd left because he'd "missed" his shot, and punctured the body of the back of the van. And that round wasn't made of silver. The bullet was normal, and hard enough to pierce the sheet metal of the van, but surrounding it was a softer nanotechnology that somehow or another Gideon could track. He left the gadgets to the Society's science and technology department. It was amazing how far technology had come since he first became a hunter.

The location of the Smoky Mountain Pack pinged reassuringly across a monitor installed beneath the dashboard of his truck.

He got tired of smiling, and dropped it.

After all this time, he was finally going to take enough of them out to make a difference. After so many decades, he was going to avenge Amalie and all the senseless deaths that had preceded and followed hers.

He was going to make his mark in the war against beasts. He was going to make the world safe for humanity again. Nestled in the depths of the Smoky Mountains, they couldn't hide anymore. Believing they were safe there, they wouldn't abandon their homes. And he wouldn't do a thing to force his hand prematurely. He'd do discreet reconnaissance. He'd assemble a team that knew what it was doing. They'd pack all the techie advantages the Society could give them and then they'd attack in the middle of the day when the wolves were at their weakest. He'd leave a few alive to question. Because everyone talked eventually.

Once he finished with the Smoky Mountain Pack, he'd go on to the next one, and then the one after that. He'd leave this world better than he found it. He'd carve out a place where people like Amalie and a younger Gideon could fall in love, have a family, and raise their children to do the same.

He owed it to Amalie. He owed it to himself.

All the years he dedicated to the cause couldn't have been for nothing. All the sacrifices he made had to mean something. The Smoky Mountain Pack was going down. He'd prepare as much as he needed to in order to make sure that once he led an attack against them, no monster would survive.

CHAPTER FIFTEEN
ZASHA

A COUPLE OF DAYS PASSED, and yet Ty and Kisha showed no signs of transforming into their human forms. Though Zasha knew next to nothing about what was usual for wolf shifters, everyone else that circulated through the infirmary was evidently alarmed.

"They must've given them enough of this Wolf Woofer to all but kill them," Quannah said on a growl that every other wolf in the room responded to. Even the feminine Chenoa, who looked as if she belonged in a rocking chair cradling an infant, her long dark hair billowing softly in a breeze that wouldn't dare be too strong for her, let loose a wicked snarl.

Ty and Kisha responded most violently. Their hackles rose, and their lips curled to expose sharp teeth. Even so, their desire to be free of the drug did nothing to hurry things along.

It wasn't until the third day since their arrival at wherever the Smoky Mountain Pack's home was located, which Zasha assumed was somewhere within the vast Great Smokies, that the drug finally wore off.

Zasha hadn't moved from her perch atop the wolf bed more often than to eat and limp outside to relieve herself. Her injuries had set in with an all-encompassing ache, but Chenoa had done a fine job of suturing her many wounds. What had her hurting the most was the dark magic that continued to pump through her veins. She wished she could speak and ask the shifters if this was common, if she was supposed to be able to feel the darkness pulsing through her body as if it were acid trying to dissolve everything that had ever been her.

But then, even if she could talk, they might not have answers for her. The one thing she'd heard over and over again over the last three days was that people like her, people made into monsters with dark magic, weren't supposed to survive. Not ever.

Of course, the wolves didn't call her a monster, though many of them looked at her with pity. But not Quannah. He looked only at her with curiosity, with wonder that shone from those deep, dark eyes of his.

The beta was recovering on pace with the rest of them. None of their injuries were common, nor did they fall under the purview of a wolf shifter's advanced supernatural healing.

Quannah lay in bed nearly as still as she did in hers, though it was obvious the brawny man was itching to get moving. When he didn't, Zasha understood that the threat to his life was more serious even than they let on within the confines of the infirmary.

How could these creatures be so strong in so many ways, she wondered, and yet nearly die over a single silver bullet? But she didn't wonder for long. Soon, she was riveted, and nothing short of her tail on fire would have moved her from her spot.

At first, she didn't understand what was happening. She whined, trying to alert Silver or one of the women who attended the wolves with him. She should have known what was happening, but the sight seemed too horrific, the sounds too brutal for it to be anything normal.

Rooted to the spot, Zasha watched Ty's large wolf head shift in shape with a crunch that made her insides twist. When the thick gray fur that covered his head tore apart, exposing red, bare flesh, nausea swept through her in a tsunami, and she had to swallow repeatedly to keep the meager contents of her stomach down.

It only got worse from there.

Seemingly all at once, the fur all across his body split in bursts, only to get sucked beneath the emerging raw flesh with a loud and stomach-churning squelch.

"Ty's finally changing," Quannah called out into the infirmary, though Chenoa, Roan, Kisha, and Zasha were already watching. Silver came running from somewhere in the back behind his alchemical corner.

Ty's transformation sped up, and Kisha scurried further out of his way.

His back split open down the middle, the vertebrae of his spine popping apart like corks on a champagne bottle.

Zasha couldn't look away as the length of his body stretched and elongated, warping every which way. All at once, too much began to happen at the same time, that she couldn't keep track of the many ways the body of a wolf had to transform to become a man. Even so, she tried to keep track of every single step, hoping it would lodge in her subconscious and lead her own body through a similar change.

When he let loose a heart-wrenching cry that was half scream, half howl, she forced herself not to retreat from what was happening to his body.

And then, both after an eternity and faster than

seemed possible, pink tender human skin coated the raw flesh, which continued on to an olive tone, sickly pale, no doubt thanks to the Pound's royal treatment.

He stood, hunched in on himself, panting, before sinking unceremoniously to the floor. Buck naked, he didn't seem to care about his nudity, catching his breath before turning to look up at Quannah.

"Well, that was fucking brutal. Must've been the drug." He sucked in deep, shaky breaths, each one growing steadier.

Silver knelt next to him. "How're you feeling, other than that nasty shift?"

Ty raked a hand through his hair; it was a thick brown that looked nothing like the color of his fur. "I feel like a Mack truck plowed into me, but I'll live. And just as soon as I've recovered my full strength, I have a Pound to burn to the ground."

His smile was vicious. Zasha had no doubt he intended to follow through. She wanted to tell him: "Don't you dare raze that place without me." But ... no mouth. Again, it sucked.

Despite Ty's protests, Quannah told him to lie down, and Silver guided the newly turned man onto the bed next to the beta's and set about examining him all over. When Silver seemed in no hurry to cover the naked man, Quannah said: "Come on, man, put a sheet over him. None of us need to look at that any more than necessary."

Ty flexed the muscles of his chest and thighs, though that definitely wasn't the part in question. "Aw, come on, Quannah, why would you do that to Ro? You know seeing me naked is the highlight of her month. Let her admire my ... equipment a bit more. Maybe she'll finally decide to overcome her shyness and come over to the wild side, AKA my bed."

Roan, who was an inch shorter even than Zasha, leaned farther into the empty bed she'd been leaning against and crossed her arms. She snorted. "The wild side? Seriously, Ty? Is that the best you can come up with to woo me into your bed? You're going to have to do better than that to convince me to overlook the deficiencies in your ... what did you call it ... equipment."

The mischief twinkling through her eyes made them glow a bright green.

Ty scoffed. "There's nothing wrong with my equipment and you know it. You're just scared of taking on the big guy. Not sure if you can handle it."

Roan's freckled cheeks spread in an evil grin. Zasha leaned forward slightly to make sure she caught whatever the fiery ginger was going to lob at him next. Whatever it was, Zasha was sure it was going to be a good one.

"Enough, you two," Quannah said, and Roan clamped her lips shut. "You can take that up in your own time."

Both Ty and Roan opened their mouths. Quannah silenced them with a glare from where he rested against two pillows and a tilted bed. "We have far more pressing matters to discuss than the sexual tension you two have been stewing since forever."

Chenoa chuckled melodically from her seat in a chair between both beds, at the head of them. "Since forevvvvvvver. They're going to explode once they finally give in."

"Guaranteed," Silver muttered jovially, continuing to examine Ty like he was lying in a life-sized Petri dish.

"Will you just cover him up already?" Quannah growled, but his eyes weren't on any of the other wolves, and certainly not on Ty's impressive package. They were on Zasha, who'd been busy reconciling what Chenoa had said with her angelic face.

When she noticed his attention, she wanted to say: "Don't worry about me, I'm no prude."

Quannah's gaze lingered on her a little too long, and by the time he released his hold on her, Silver had covered Ty in a sheet—which tented slightly. Zasha didn't dare look and draw Quannah's attention there.

His voice grumbly, Quannah turned his head to see Ty. "Tell us what happened. All of it. We looked for you for over three months, until we finally found you."

Ty blanched at the mention of how long it had been, making his pasty complexion go sallow.

"Hold up," Silver interjected. "What have they been feeding you? Quannah, he might need to eat before he can get into it."

"If he had it in him to tease Ro, he can talk," Quannah said, but it didn't sound like an order, more like a question.

Ty nodded gently, as if he had a killer headache. "I wouldn't mind a shower either. The Pound feels like it's stuck to me. But I've got it in me to tell you what went down."

Zasha leaned so far in her bed that she ended up having to scoot down farther. It wasn't that the proximity would help her hear better; she could already hear more than was comfortable when compared to her human hearing. She could hear every heart beating within the room, the boiling of several liquids over in Silver's alchemical corner, and hear the easy breathing of all the uninjured shifters, along with the labored breathing of the rest of them, including hers. She could hear the leaves swaying in the trees outside, the birds chirping, and a chipmunk burying a nut. She had no idea how she was so certain it was a chipmunk instead of, say, a squirrel, but she was, her nose twitching in confirmation.

The reason she leaned forward to ensure she didn't miss a word, a nuance, or a reaction, was because she hoped therein lay the secret to her recovery.

If dark magic hadn't killed her yet when it should have, maybe she could somehow find her way back to her human self—and from there to the life she was snatched from.

"When they took us," Ty started, "Kisha, Moore, and me, it was no accident." He tilted his head to look at his beta. "They didn't find us by chance. It was an ambush. They were waiting for us."

"But no one knew you were going to be there but Corin, Flynn, and me." Quannah trailed off as he seemed to go elsewhere to consider what that might mean. Zasha wondered if that meant they had a mole among them, but without any real knowledge as to how the pack worked, it was only a guess.

Before Quannah could prompt him to continue, Ty did.

"You know how we were supposed to go check out a couple of rogue wolves, right?" He faced Quannah, who nodded. "Well, when we finally found them, running around in the forest outside of Asheville, they weren't rogue wolves at all."

Kisha whined, but Zasha didn't look at her, unable to pull away from the meaningful stare Ty shared with their beta.

"They were wolves made from dark magic, totally out of their minds. One of the wolves, poor bastard, couldn't even run in a straight line. It was like his motor functioning was off. He kept tripping over his own legs, landing on his face and dragging himself up."

Ty glanced at Kisha for a quick moment. "The other wolf was a bit better off, but not by much. He might've been worse. He looked crazy." Ty circled his eyes with an index finger. "His eyes..." He shook his head. "Whatever was going on up there, it was bad, really bad."

Ty frowned and shrugged. "We figured the best was to take them out."

"Put them out of their misery," Chenoa added. "It was the right thing to do, don't you think, Quannah?"

"Definitely. No one survives a forced shift with black magic."

As one, they all looked at Zasha, who flared her nostrils at them in silent defiance. If there was going to be one who did, it was going to be her.

"Anyway," Ty said, "the three of us shifted to take them out fast and give them a good end. But when we got to them..." He stopped to shake his head, then frowned, his eyes suddenly turning murderous, glowing violet. "It was a setup. There were a half dozen of them. Had they played by the rules, we could have taken them down. You know"—he swallowed—"Moore, Kish, and me, we could've taken 'em down even two to one. But they didn't use guns. They used magic on us."

Roan muttered something under her breath that Zasha wished she'd understood. She thought it might be Gaelic. Whatever language she was speaking, no doubt she was cussing up a storm, and Zasha mightily wanted to join in.

Ty pinned murderous eyes on Quannah, but it was as if he were lookin' straight through him. "Not all of them had magic, only two of them, but it was enough. They froze us where we stood and then we had to watch while one of the assholes shot us up with enough of this drug to take down a whole pack. Whatever else they did to us, we didn't wake up again until we were in the cells at the bottom of the Pound. And we couldn't use the pack link, or shift, or anything. And when they started beating us to get us to do what they wanted, we couldn't heal worth a shit either."

"I'm gonna kill them," Roan growled, sounding like a wolf for the first time.

"I get it, guys," Quannah said. "Trust me, I do. I want to blow the place up with everyone inside it like it's a firework show. But we have to wait for Corin. He has to decide what we do about this."

"And when's he coming back?" Roan asked, pushing off of the bed she leaned against as if she would go to the Pound to deliver a beatdown right this second.

"He should be back by now, so he'll be here soon. But we'll need a plan before we go barging in there."

"But—" Roan said.

"I don't want to leave anyone behind when we do go in," Quannah said. "Anyone that supports forcing wolves to shift or pitting them against each other in a ring like that deserves to die."

"Hell yeah they do," Silver said.

"They might move the location of the Pound if we wait too long," Ty said.

"I know." Quannah rubbed a hand over his face, sighing loudly. "Fuck, I know. And no way are we letting that asshole in the VIP box slip through our fingers. But Corin's almost here, and that's a big operation to move."

Silence.

Quannah's shoulders fell. "They've probably

already moved the mystery VIP man anyway. They would've done it as soon as we broke you guys out. We'll be lucky to find much of anything left by the time we get there. But I can't risk the pack like that when there's no imminent threat. You know the rules."

They might, but Zasha sure as hell didn't.

"We keep under the radar as much as possible, because our main mission is to make the world safe from the hunters for all supernatural creatures," Ty said.

"Exactly," Quannah said, though his jaw was tight as though the solution weren't satisfying to him either. "We can't risk the mission. If we don't take the hunters out, they'll never stop tracking us. Supes will never be safe if we don't succeed."

"But they won't be safe either so long as places like the Pound exist," Roan said.

Quannah's brows were dark, severe lines. "Agreed. We had to get our wolves out first, and now we'll just do the best we can. Even if they've packed up the Pound, we'll find them again. Those kinds of people don't stop what they're doin' for long."

Zasha grunted, drawing the beta's gaze. She was still going to light the place up like a blowtorch, whether they were there anymore or not.

"And what about our she-wolf?" Quannah asked Ty. "What do you know about her?"

But before Ty could answer, Kisha let out a pained yip, and then her own transformation began. It was as hideous and prolonged as Ty's.

Zasha barely breathed while she watched, wondering what her turn would be like, or if she'd ever get a turn.

CHAPTER SIXTEEN

QUANNAH

KISHA'S SHIFT was as brutal as Ty's, which wasn't normal for either one of the shifters.

"It must be the drugs," Silver said, voicing his exact thought.

"And by that I hope you mean we won't have to endure that crazy shit again," Ty said from the bed next to Quannah. "Really makes me feel for the weres."

The wolf had settled down since his blatant flirtation with Roan. Sexual tension between the two shifters wasn't new, but Quannah knew Ty well enough to understand most of it had been for show, a distraction from what he was actually feeling. That man didn't do fear or weakness. And being locked up in a place like the Pound ... well, had it been Quannah, the confinement would have driven him crazy. He didn't do cages. Few wolves could.

Together, he, Silver, Ty, Chenoa, and Roan watched Kisha finish her transformation. The she-wolf watched too, her eyes wide as she trained on every abrupt change in Kisha's body.

Most of the shifters in their pack possessed enough natural magic to shift without pain. It wasn't anything they could control or train for; either they had enough magic or they didn't. Those who didn't endured sufficient discomfort with each shift to choose not to transform more often than necessary. And then there were the werewolves. Those poor bastards suffered through each shift and there was no getting out of it. During the three days when the moon was at its fullest, they became wolves. Their pained howls could be heard for miles around as their animal natures consumed them.

It was why the Smoky Mountain Pack never made wolves. It was forbidden. No one should have such a drastic change forced upon them.

Quannah's gaze drifted from Kisha, nearly fully human now, to the she-wolf. Her body, with all its visible sutures, was tense as she took in the transformation. Bare patches of flesh peeked through the unusual yellow-hued fur, revealing that the she-wolf was healing despite whatever the black magic was doing inside her.

How was she even still alive? he wondered, and far from the first time.

Corin would be fascinated by her once he met her. The thought sent an uncomfortable twinge racing through him, making him pause and peer at the wolf even more closely.

She noticed, turning piercing blue eyes on him that were free of the violet streaks that were a signature of their pack. He froze, locked in her stare for a few moments before remembering that he was the dominant wolf and that she should look away.

Only she didn't. She seemed to slam her will against his.

So, amid the final grunts of Kisha's completing shift, he shoved back, pushing the force of his energy against hers. Still, she didn't look away, though he sensed that she was struggling to maintain her stare.

He sat up further against his pillows, careful as ever not to move his shoulder more than necessary, and prepared to leach out some of his power, not so much to assert dominance anymore but to test her.

Kisha growled. Though in her human form, she sounded like she was still in her wolf body, and the she-wolf turned to look at her.

Quannah didn't. He continued to watch the she-wolf, more curious about the creature than ever.

"Those fuckers are gonna pay for what they did to us," Kisha roared.

The she-wolf didn't even flinch at the woman's fury or volume.

"Come on, Kish." Silver patted the last empty human bed in the infirmary. "You should rest."

"Rest? Are you kidding me right now, Silver? Do you know what they did to us in that place? What they did to Moore?"

"What did they do to Moore?" Quannah asked quietly, finally looking at the shifter with the wild corkscrew curls of dark hair. He didn't really want to know, but as beta he had to find out, especially since Corin was still away.

Kisha wheeled on Quannah, once more ignoring Silver's attempts to coax her into a bed. "They forced him to kill wolves who were all messed up in the head. They forced him to fight us. And when he refused to take me down in the ring like they asked, they killed him. They bloody killed him!"

Quannah had known Kisha all of her life as well. The shifter was hiding behind her rage, and he wouldn't stop her.

"They caged us, they hurt us, and they made us do things we should never have to do. Whoever the bastard is that runs the place, I'm killing him." She shook her head and brought her hands to her waist, her wild, wide eyes and hair sticking straight out on all sides more than usual making her look crazed. "Nope, I'm not just killing him. I'm going to rip his balls off and feed them to him. Then, I'm going to let him bleed out."

"As long as I get to watch," Ty said, but both shifters were just blowing hot air. Not that they wouldn't want to punish the man responsible for doing this to them, but because no one made a move as big as that one without the alpha's say-so, and the Smoky Mountain Pack never killed without need. That was a firm rule, one which Quannah wondered if Corin would be willing to throw out the window under these circumstances.

"Do you know the name of the guy in the VIP box?" Quannah asked.

"No," Kisha said. "But when we go after him, his balls are mine. On a platter."

Quannah just nodded and glanced at the she-wolf again. The wolf looked unperturbed by Kisha's outburst.

Silver patted the empty bed once more. "Come on. Lie down. I need to make sure you're okay."

"I'll be okay once I dismember that prick." She growled again. "Do you know what they called me there? What my 'call name' was? It was Black Rack. *Black Rack.*" She waved a hand along her naked body, cupping her breasts. "Not too creative, those fuckers."

Then she stomped her black, beautiful ass over to the bed and jumped onto it, shooting Silver a glare when she caught him checking out said naked behind.

Kisha was beautiful, no doubt about it, but she was a powder keg. If Silver was going to go there, he'd better wait until she was less combustible. She lay her head down on the pillow and allowed Silver to examine her before also covering her with a sheet.

"I'm black and have tits, so they called me Black Rack," she muttered, before meeting eyes with Quannah, who had to drag his attention away from the she-wolf.

"People like that don't deserve to live."

"We'll see what Corin wants to do once he gets here."

"And when does he get here?" Kisha asked.

"Soon. He said he'd be back here by this evening."

"Good. Even Corin will be able to see that this is a time for exceptions and kicking ass."

"I get it, Kish," Quannah said, "I really do."

"We all do," Roan said, walking over to give

Kisha a hug through the sheet. "We looked for you guys everywhere. We had no idea where you'd gone. Chenoa even consulted the elders."

"They couldn't see you," Chenoa said. "They said it was black around you."

Ty's nostrils flared. "The dark magic. Had to be."

"How many dark mages did they have?" Quannah asked, itching to get up and pace. After three days of bed rest, he was ready to never lie down again. But he owed it to his pack to take it easy. Besides, if he got up, Silver wouldn't stop hounding him until he lay back down again. It wasn't worth it.

"They had three mages," Ty said, and the she-wolf snapped her head up to look at him.

Quannah noticed. It seemed he couldn't help but notice everything the she-wolf did. She had something to say about the mages but no way to say it. Even without the dark magic running through her, she wouldn't have been able to access their pack link. It was only for members of the Smoky Mountain Pack, and that was something she could never be. She was unlikely to live long enough, and besides, the magic that coursed through her was akin to poison. Corin would never allow a wolf created by black magic to join the pack.

No matter what happened to her, her fate wouldn't be entwined with his.

With theirs, he corrected. With the pack's.

She wasn't his.

Wasn't his *problem*, he adjusted once more, wondering if his mind was still sluggish due to the silver poisoning.

With sudden awareness, he realized the others were watching him ... watch her.

"The guy in the VIP box you were asking about," Ty finally continued, "he's one of them. And then there were two others that I noticed. You, Kish?"

She pushed away Silver's hand as he attempted to shine a penlight in her eyes. "Just the three, though maybe there were some other minor players with some magic. It was hard to tell since I can't sense magic the way others can."

Then Kisha took in the she-wolf, gesturing toward her with her chin. "She bit one of their faces pretty bad. I could smell her on him, even through the antiseptic."

"She definitely held her own in the ring too," Ty said. "Though she shouldn't have been able to."

Quannah eyed the she-wolf once more, eager to discuss her performance in the ring, when Kisha sat straight up—before wobbling and sinking back down.

"Dammit, Kisha," Silver said. "You act like nothing happened to you, but you were drugged and held in a fucking dungeon for three long months. Will you chill the fuck out already?"

"I'll chill out when Ty explains why he took her side over mine out in the ring." Even if her outburst hadn't been accompanied by a weak growl, it would still have been an obvious accusation.

"I had to, Kish," Ty said, running a tired hand through his hair before letting it plop loudly to the bed beside him. "You were going to kill her."

"I had to kill her. It wasn't because I wanted to. It was the only way to survive."

"I was trying to tell you there was another way with this one, but you wouldn't listen. What else was I supposed to do?"

"You were supposed to have your packmate's back, no matter what. That's what you were supposed to do. That's what you're always supposed to do. Defend me if I need help."

"You didn't need help. You were about to kill her. And when you did need help, I kept her off you."

"Yeah, well, I failed to notice."

"Maybe because you were crazed and not thinking straight."

"Not thinking straight? Seriously, Ty? What the hell? After all we've been through, you want to defend a wolf who's going to die anyway instead of me? Killing her was a mercy kill. *Mercy*, not crazed bloodlust, you get that?"

Quannah was preparing to step in. The wolves would have to get this out in the open at some point, but it didn't have to be now, not so soon after their first shifts back. Now that they'd kicked the drugs out of their system, their healing would kick in and they'd be back to themselves in no time.

But before Quannah could say anything, Ty said: "She could have killed me and she didn't, okay? She had a kill shot, and that fucking announcer was even egging her on. But she didn't take it."

Chenoa stopped rocking in her chair and leaned forward. Roan moved to Ty's side, slapping him softly on the arm. "Blimey, don't just leave us hanging. What the bloody hell happened? Why did the she-wolf have to help you?"

"I refused to fight." He shrugged, but his voice was as tumultuous as a raging river. "They'd already taken away food and water, and that didn't work, so they started threatening me by hurting Moore."

"You should've just fought," Kisha said. "It was easier that way, and it would've spared Moore."

Ty whipped his head in her direction so fast his neck cracked. "You think I realized they'd hurt Moore to get to me? Who the hell do you think I am, Kisha? It's like you don't fucking know me at all."

"You didn't have my back out in the ring."

"That's not true and you know it." He glared at her so ferociously that Kisha finally had the grace to appear repentant, but she quickly wiped the apologetic grimace from her face.

Ty looked back at the she-wolf, and Quannah followed. She stared back at both of them.

"When you came to get us," Ty said, "they were using the stock prods on me."

"Those weren't plain cattle prods," Kisha interjected. "They were suped-up hot sticks. They had enough juice in them to take down a herd of elephants."

"Yeah, they stung, no doubt," Ty went on, still staring at the she-wolf, who held his eyes. "They buzzed me so hard I could barely move. And then the announcer basically told her to take the kill." He smiled at the she-wolf, and Quannah felt the insane urge to throw himself between the two of them.

"She didn't take it. She licked my wounds clean and tried to get me to defend myself when Kisha came in the ring instead."

"Only I would never be against you in a fight," Kisha snapped.

"But the she-wolf didn't know that when she tried to protect me, now did she? And I didn't hurt you. I took you down but I didn't use teeth. I just wanted you to give her a chance to try to get out of there. And see? We all made it out."

"But you didn't know—"

"Enough," Quannah said, and Kisha pursed her lips closed, eyes still narrowed at Ty, who didn't appear to care.

"Any idea who the she-wolf is or how come she's still breathing?" Quannah asked.

"None," Ty said. "She's right. They only brought her in the day before you got us out of there. And she was completely knocked out when they brought her by."

"They brought her in with some others," Kisha said. "Four of them."

"And what happened to them?" Quannah asked.

"The usual. Dead. Pitted against each other in the ring, or against one of us, whatever. They always end up dead."

"They don't usually last more than a day or two," Ty said, curious. "I ended some because you could almost see the dark magic tearing them apart inside. There was no coming back from that for them."

"And for her?" Quannah wondered aloud. "Can she come back from this?"

"If she's made it this far," Silver said, "who knows? But ... don't get your hopes up. It's unlikely.

We'll probably end up having to kill her to put her out of her misery."

The she-wolf snarled viciously as she rose onto her legs. Her injured front leg wobbled but held her weight. She hunched into her shoulders, her sutured chest pulled in, her ears pressed back.

"Whoa, girl," Ty said, a hand up. "No one here is gonna hurt you."

"Yet," Kisha muttered quietly, and the she-wolf snapped at her, teeth gnashing.

And then without warning, the she-wolf collapsed on her bed.

Before Quannah could consider what he was doing, his bare feet hit the floor and he jetted out of his bed and toward her.

"Quannah!" Silver warned, but Quannah barely heard him.

He reached for the she-wolf, but before his hand could reach that unusual yellow-tinged fur, it split open straight down her back and she yelped.

The she-wolf who wasn't supposed to survive or shift was doing both.

CHAPTER SEVENTEEN

QUANNAH

AS UGLY AS Ty and Kisha's shifts had been, the she-wolf's was worse. His entire body tensed up when the flesh along her back rent in two, and the tension hadn't let up since then. He was mindful not to call attention to the way his arms and stomach muscles clenched, how his legs were hard as rock. The last thing he needed was Silver breathing down his neck, telling him stress would only impede his recovery.

He couldn't help his reaction, didn't even understand why the thought of the she-wolf's suffering had his stomach churning noisily. Despite the fact that the shifts of the wolf shifters in the Smoky Mountain Pack were usually far more graceful than these, the life of a shifter wasn't without pain. Threats surrounded them on all sides. Even when they couldn't see them, they knew the hunters were just waiting for them to slip up so they could take them down. They were always watching, and danger didn't just come from them.

The Pound was one of the worst abusers of wolf shifters he'd seen in recent years. But where there was power and magic, there were always those wanting more of it, wanting to hurt others for their gain—or worse, for sport and pleasure.

Other wolf packs didn't always play nice, though Corin was a strong alpha and commanded respect, so other packs mostly left them alone now. But there were far more supernaturals than wolf shifters and werewolves. There were other types of shifters and animals that had only one form but weren't supposed to exist in the world of humans. And then there were the mages—the witches and wizards whose magic could do good as easily as it could do bad. No, risk was a part of the path they'd chosen, part of their mission to set their kind free.

Quannah was used to experiencing pain, within himself and those he cared about. There was simply no way around it. So why was every single muscle in his body clenched against the she-wolf's pain? If she managed to fully transform into a person, she might still die. Or worse...

"It's taking too long," Ty said. "What if she gets stuck in a halfway form?"

"She won't," Quannah snapped at his friend, though of course she very well could.

Her shift had gone on far too long, and still she was an unsettling mixture of skin and fur.

"It's because she's supposed to be dead by now," Kisha said, a tangible lack of emotion in her pronouncement that had Quannah clenching and unclenching his fingers before he realized it.

When Silver caught the movement, Quannah stopped.

"No wolf is supposed to be made with dark magic," Kisha went on, as if that weren't fucking obvious. "It's not the way it's done. It's not natural. That's why she can't finish her shift. Because she's not supposed to exist."

The she-wolf, twisted and writhing on the floor, unable to hold her weight on the current combination of human and wolf, whipped herself from her pain for long enough to hurl a rumbling snarl at Kisha.

"Whoa. Down, girl," Kisha said, half chuckling.

Quannah knew Kisha well, and he well knew she was about as delicate and subtle as a twin-barrel shotgun. The woman was as brash as a pimp strolling down a seedy street in Flaming Arrow, decked out in a purple-plumed hat and too much swagger.

But the she-wolf's snarl died on her half-wolf, half-woman lips, and she once more contorted in an agonized mesh of parts.

"Should we ... put her down?" Roan asked.

Quannah snapped his head in her direction so fast that Silver pressed a hand against his shoulder to keep him from moving too much. Roan put up her hands, her eyes skimming from Quannah to Ty and back to the beta. Ty was glaring too.

"I just mean, if she can't complete the shift, we can't just leave her like that. It looks ... awful."

And that it did.

"It's been too long," Chenoa said in that melodic voice of hers that somehow carried as much strength as his. "Even taking into account that she's a new wolf, her woman should have emerged by now."

No one said anything while the she-wolf's body shook and heaved, her chest, now with the suggestion of human breasts, panting from exertion. Then the she-wolf whimpered, and Quannah sucked in a sharp breath.

He couldn't let her go on like this. The women were right. If she didn't pull through this shift soon, she wouldn't, and it would be his responsibility to put an end to her torment.

She whined, and he spoke before he knew what he'd say, which wasn't his way at all.

"Fine. If she doesn't pull through soon, I'll do it."

The promise of *it* hung in the air like a dark and dense monsoon cloud.

"She'll pull through," Ty said, but his voice didn't carry the conviction it usually did. "You should've seen her in the Pound. She's a fighter. She shouldn't have been able to even stand up hardly, let alone fight, and she was fighting Kisha to keep her away from me."

Ty, still occupying the bed next to him, turned to face Quannah. "She would have had no way to know that Kisha wouldn't hurt me. She wouldn't have known we're pack mates. She'd just been made a wolf with that fucked-up nasty magic and she was trying to defend me." Ty's eyes hardened. "Me. She was trying to help me when she was probably ready to drop herself. We can't just give up on her."

"It's not about giving up," Quannah said, barely above a whisper. "It's about mercy." He sighed. "If she can't come out of this..." He shook his head. "Then she can't come out of this."

"We should've never brought her with us," Kisha started to say, and Ty snapped at her with a snarl that rivaled the she-wolf's.

Goosebumps coated Quannah's flesh in a rush

while he took in Ty and Kisha, who looked like she'd finally decided to keep her mouth shut. Knowing her, that resolve wouldn't last long. It never did. Kisha was as explosive as a powder keg during a fireworks show.

That's when he realized that it was too silent, too still.

Thinking she might be dead, he slowly dragged his gaze over to the floor next to the wolf bed she'd occupied for days. For all the days he'd been relegated to bed rest, he'd watched her—and she'd watched him, more intelligence behind those eyes than dark magic should allow.

And when his eyes finally alighted on her form, he stopped breathing. Perhaps even his heart stopped beating. It felt like everything ceased to exist in that moment beyond her.

He could tell the others around him were talking, but he couldn't focus on what they were saying.

Despite every odd that had pressed against her, the she-wolf was no longer a wolf.

She was all glorious woman.

Born into a wolf shifter family and into a large wolf pack, Quannah had been around nudity his entire life. No shifter could afford to be precious about showing skin. It was simply their way of life. Everyone had seen everyone's bits at one time or another, though etiquette dictated that one should never stare. As with humans and their urinals, one wasn't supposed to look.

But he was staring—and he couldn't get himself to stop.

The woman on the floor was still panting, still recovering from what she'd been through to complete her transformation. She hadn't even looked at any of them yet.

Her hair was long and straight, a mess beneath her in the same color as that odd gold tone that shone from the underlayer of her wolf's fur. Her body was firm all over, long, lean muscles indenting her flesh. No bulk anywhere. Even her breasts were perky and not particularly large. Her pubic zone was dusted in that same dark blond hair. When he caught himself staring, he quickly looked away ... his gaze landing on her face.

Even with her eyes closed, he leaned forward in the bed, trying to get closer to her despite the divide between them. Her lips were slightly parted with evident exhaustion ... or maybe relief. But to him they appeared parted in pleasure, and the baser part of his anatomy stirred, alarming him.

He ordered it to obey his will and continued studying her smooth, milky skin, peppered in scars; her straight, pleasant nose; curved eyebrows slightly darker than her hair, and dark, thick lashes resting along her cheeks, which indented beneath her cheekbones. Her lips were bright and bowed. His body tried to stir again and he clamped a mental hold on it.

Down, he ordered, and his body partially responded.

"I can't believe it," Roan was saying, and Quannah finally made out words, but then the she-wolf opened her eyes and met his, and the world faded away again.

Her eyes were a deep, crystalline blue, big and round, as innocent-looking as her bowed, cherry mouth. Only the rest of her didn't suggest she was innocent. Her body was hard as if she trained as much as their pack did. Deep within her eyes, where his stare reached, there was nothing soft about her.

She pushed onto her elbows, the expanding of her rib cage slowing as she caught her breath. Her eyes boring into his, she said: "Take a picture, why don't you? It'll last longer."

Her voice was deep and smoky, like a saxophone weaving its music around a dimly lit nightclub, when the night was full of seedy promise and the whiskey was poured straight.

He kicked up a knee so the sheet pulled away from his crotch.

Slowly he became aware of the silence that

followed her statement. The others would be waiting for him to speak first. They didn't always remember he was their beta. Most of them were raised together; sometimes they forgot he wasn't just their friend, but their leader. But when the circumstances were shocking enough, they always remembered.

He cleared his throat, working to shake the uncomfortable feeling that he was a prepubescent teen again working to control rogue boners. He was the beta of one of the most important packs in North America. He needed to act like it.

He ignored her lingering question which poked at his unwelcome reaction to her.

"Roan, will you please get the she-wolf some clothes?"

Once Roan started rummaging through a supply closet, he added: "And a change of sheets. She can have my bed."

Silver went rigid, shaking his head. "Quannah, please, you have to rest."

"I've done nothing but rest for days. Surely by now my body has expelled enough of the silver for my wolf healing to kick in and do the rest."

"But it has to have expelled all the silver. Every bit of it."

When Quannah pushed to sit up all the way,

Silver fluttered his hands around him as if to try to keep him there, and Silver wasn't the fluttery sort.

Quannah was torn between wanting to beat his chest to the tune of his masculinity like a silverback gorilla, and being dutiful to his responsibilities as the pack's second-in-command. If something happened to him, sure, Flynn would replace him, and Flynn was a capable leader. But Quannah was better, and he knew it.

His pack needed him.

He sighed, working not to be annoyed by Silver's panic. He, too, only wanted what was best for their pack.

"How about we compromise?" Quannah told their equivalent of a physician. "I'll sit in that recliner over there."

"I can leave my bed for the she-wolf," Ty piped up. "I'm feeling much better already."

"Well, you look like shit," Quannah said. "You need to keep resting. Doesn't he, Silver?"

Silver looked between all of them, clearly trying to keep them all in bed as long as possible. Silver was a ferocious fighter when he had to be, but when he didn't, he was a mother hen.

Before Silver could decide whom he wanted to keep in bed more, the she-wolf spoke: "I'm no delicate flower," she said, drawing everyone's attention back to her.

Roan hustled over to her with a pair of surgical scrubs that the infirmary kept on hand in all sizes. The she-wolf received them with a curt smile of thanks.

"I'm perfectly fine recovering here on the floor. I won't need long anyway."

"Of course you will," Silver said right away. "You'll probably need longer than everyone else here. Look at you. Your arm and chest are still hanging open. You need fresh stitches."

Quannah had barely noticed the large cuts, which had healed quite a bit despite Silver's panic. The beta had noticed everything else.

"Besides," Silver said, "that magic you have coursing through you is a problem. A big problem. Like, massive. You can't just brush that off."

Quannah expected the she-wolf to argue. She didn't.

He studied her, scanning her face as she dressed.

Roan hadn't given her underwear, so the she-wolf slipped pants and shirt on quickly. Her nipples pressed against the plain-blue thin cotton, transforming the lumpy scrubs into something erotic. She didn't seem to care, though his body did, dammit.

She pulled her hair out of her shirt and slid to

lean against the wall, bringing one knee up, her injured arm hanging carefully over it.

"Look," she started, "I'll take it easy, okay? I know how to look out for myself. But don't worry. I won't be here long anyway. As soon as I feel strong enough, I'm out of here."

Tension rolled through Quannah again, pinching his shoulders.

"You will not leave here until you heal," he ordered, his nostrils flaring.

She scoffed. "You can't make me stay here."

"Oh yes I can. You won't leave here until I say so." As an afterthought, he added: "Or the alpha says so."

He felt the others looking at him curiously, probably wondering what the hell was wrong with him, just as he was. It was like he couldn't help himself.

"So, what, I'm your prisoner now?" she asked, the hint of a threat riding the question.

"No, you aren't."

"But I can't leave?"

"No, you can't. Glad you're catching on."

Her nostrils flared at him this time, and hell if it didn't make his groin heat.

"We can help you."

"From what you've been saying, none of you knows what to make of me. According to y'all, I wasn't supposed to live or shift to human, so what do you know?"

His voice came out as a low growl. "Silver can figure it out. He and Chenoa and Roan will help you."

"So long as I stay here."

"You have to stay." Quannah didn't like the hint of desperation that crept into his voice. He cleared his throat again, as if that would help. Something was wrong with him.

She stared him down for so long he didn't think she would speak. He stared right back at her, growing more annoyed by the second.

"I have to get back to my family," she finally said. "They'll be looking for me."

"There is no going back," he said. "You might as well be dead to your family."

It came out harsher than he'd intended, but he didn't take it back.

"We'll see about that," she said.

"I guess we will."

And then those blue eyes seared into his until he gasped.

"That's not possible."

"What's not possible?" Silver asked right away.

"Probably the crazy tension between them that you could slice," Kisha said with her signature snark, but softly enough that it wouldn't be interpreted as defying her beta.

Quannah ignored her, croaking out: "Her eyes."

He swallowed thickly. "It's not possible."

Only it was.

There was no denying the grayish violet that streaked through her blue irises, the violet pulsing, coming alive before his very eyes.

"No way," Ty said on a breath of barely-there air.

"It shouldn't be possible," Quannah repeated. But that didn't change a thing.

CHAPTER EIGHTEEN

ZASHA

GREAT, now something was wrong with her eyes too. Was anything right with her anymore?

She was going to murder Marley. And then she was going to roast Mystery Boss Man on a blazing spit, nice and slowly.

Every single person in the room was staring at her. Even that Kisha chick, who'd barely stopped glaring at her for a second, was looking at her in a new kind of way. Her mouth hung open, transforming the usually hard expressions of her face into something approachable. Zasha doubted it would last long.

She decided to wait them out. Surely they'd realize they were being rude assholes at some point and stop their gawking. When that didn't happen, she snapped: "What? What the hell could it possibly be now?"

"That's a very fine question," Chenoa said, her normally melodic voice grating against her.

"I know it's a good question. I asked it. Now what's the answer?"

Chenoa, Kisha, Roan, and Ty all turned to look at Quannah, who continued gawping at her like she'd sprouted a third eye.

With a start, he seemed to come into some self-awareness. "I'll need to speak with Corin about this."

"I've gathered that Corin is your pack's alpha, but what is 'this?'"

When he still didn't answer, and the anticipation grew to become a tangible force in the air, she sighed. "Look ... I've been through hell and back, possibly literally. I'm in no mood to play games with you. Tell me what I need to know so I can figure out what's going on with me and I can be on my way."

When he still hesitated, she said: "Or don't tell me, whatever. But don't expect to hold me here against my will. I'll leave and figure out what's going on all on my own."

She went to fling her hands in the air—a habitual mannerism—and winced. Damn, she'd forgotten that while she'd healed some her skin was indeed still hanging open, and it hurt worse than getting punched in the face by Big Tommy, and he was six-foot-three and all muscle and little brains. His right hook was wicked.

While she waited for an explanation, she hoped the beta wouldn't call what had become her bluff. She'd really rather one of the tending wolf shifters stitch her up again before going anywhere. She wouldn't make it far in this kind of shape.

Quannah made her wait while he batted away the protests of Silver and made his way over to the recliner. He moved just fine. He moved like a fighter.

While his back was turned to her, she studied him, not caring that Kisha, Ty, Chenoa, and Roan were staring. If they were going to ogle, so was she.

All of the wolf shifters in the room were fit. So Quannah's long muscles weren't particularly unique, but on him they were particularly scrumptious.

He was barefoot in slightly worn bootcut jeans. He'd skipped a belt, and wore nothing more than a plain black t-shirt that rose as he bent over to adjust the tilt of the recliner, causing Silver to all but hyperventilate at whatever minimal effort the beta was making. Zasha, however, was all for the motions that revealed a band of toned abdomen and waist that was a mix between her pale skin and Kisha's dark mocha. A dusting of dark hair paved the path to the promised land.

"Take a picture, why don't you?" he said, smirking at her. "It'll last longer."

Shit. She hadn't even noticed how hard she'd been staring.

She smirked at her words thrown back at her. "Thought you might like to know what it feels like."

When he smiled, revealing bright, straight teeth, he looked every bit the predator.

She had to work not to squirm, and not because she wanted to run away. More like she had to keep herself from doing something crazy like going and jumping on the stranger's lap.

"Oh for fuck's sake," Kisha grumbled. "Want us to vacate the room?" She tossed her head, her thick wild curls bouncing.

Quannah leveled a ferocious look on her that shut her right up, then he faced Zasha.

"Your eyes are changing. That's why we were all staring."

Sure, buddy, sure, Zasha thought. His gaze hadn't remained on her eyes.

She frowned and turned to watch Roan strip Quannah's bed of its sheets and industriously sheath it in fresh ones.

"What do you mean my eyes are changing?" Hesitantly, unsure she wanted to know what exactly that meant, she felt her eye sockets. "They ... feel okay."

She tamped down a mini-wave of panic. "Am I going to ... lose them or something?" She wasn't sure she could handle losing another thing after losing her papa and her humanity. Surely she'd find the way to endure it if she had to, but got busy hoping she wouldn't have to.

"Nothing's wrong with your eyes," Quannah said, and relief whooshed through her like a fierce wind.

"Do we really know that though?" Kisha said. "She has black magic in her. *Black magic*. Anything could be happening to her right now."

"Is your nickname Killjoy, by any chance?" Zasha asked her.

"I do what I have to do to protect this pack. Pack first," she added, with a quick glare under thick lashes at Ty. "The way I see it, you're a threat to all of us."

"And the way I see it, you're a raging bitch," Zasha said, not stopping to consider the wisdom of it. She'd just lost her father; she'd been kidnapped, beaten, and made into a beast. And now she was being held prisoner by a whole bunch of monstery people. She wasn't in the mood to control her temper; she wasn't even sure she had the spare energy for it.

Kisha was busy growling at her. "What did you just say to me?"

Zasha rubbed a hand over her face, using the arm that didn't have a flap of loose flesh hanging from it. "Look ... I've been through some *shit* the last several days. Just, give me a break, okay? You aren't a raging bitch."

Kisha was, however, definitely a bitch, just without the raging part.

"You've been trying to kill me or get me killed since I first saw you. What do you expect?"

"It's nothing personal," Kisha said. "I don't even know you."

Zasha smiled tightly, like she'd just swallowed a bug. "It's pretty damn personal when you're talking about killing me."

Roan walked over to her, offering a genuine smile that lit up the redhead's face. Grateful, Zasha smiled back.

"Let's get you into bed," Roan said, and Zasha allowed her to lead her to the freshly made bed that was still warm from Quannah's body heat. She settled into it, allowing it to soothe her and not questioning why it did.

While Silver collected the tools he'd need to sew her up again, Quannah said, "It's true that we don't know what to expect with you. You've heard us talking about you and the dark magic used to transform you." His voice was a steady, deep bass that vibrated through her body to her core.

She nodded.

"I'd like to hear more about it. Maybe it will help us understand what's happening to you."

"Fine." She could use all the help she could get for sure. "But first, what the hell is going on with my eyes?"

While holding her gaze with an unflinching steadiness that made Zasha understand why this man was the beta of this wolf pack, Quannah said: "Your eyes are beginning to look like ours. This is the Smoky Mountain Pack, and when a wolf becomes a part of the pack, their eyes shift, adopting the violet streaks you've no doubt noticed in all of us."

She nodded. "Of course I noticed."

"Well, your eyes currently have violet streaks too."

"Okay." She shrugged. "But that's not a big deal, right? I mean, when I leave, the streaks will go away."

No one said anything for a beat.

"Right?" she pressed.

"Probably not."

"Why not? I'm not a member of your pack."

"You haven't been inducted into the pack, but your eyes say differently."

"But ... why?"

Quannah shook his head, his shoulder-length black hair reflecting the overhead lights.

"I don't know. Ordinarily, only the alpha can induct new wolves into the pack, and Corin doesn't do so lightly. Our pack is different than other packs."

"Why?"

"Because we hunt those who hunt us."

"The Pound people?"

His eyes blazed with a latent anger that illuminated the violet streaks in his dark eyes, making them appear to glow from within. "No. Another group who's been hunting us always."

"And who are they?"

"The hunters."

"And they hunt you? Um, us, I guess?"

"They do," he said.

"So what's keeping you from kicking their asses? You're wolf shifters, for fuck's sake."

"They have weapons forged in magic."

"So?" She felt her brow furrow. "You're *wolves*."

Quannah continued to stare back at her. "Generations of their kind have dedicated themselves to killing us. They have ways."

"As do we," Ty piped up.

Quannah nodded. "As do we."

"Which is why Corin doesn't induct just

anybody into the pack," Kisha said. "They have to prove themselves."

"What? Like by surviving dark magic when no one else does? Or maybe by kicking your bony ass?"

Kisha's ass was far from bony, but Zasha's words hit their intended mark. Kisha bolted out of bed.

Silver, who was disinfecting the needle he meant to use on Zasha, whirled, hands extended toward Kisha.

"Get your ass back in bed," he told her. "You're in no condition to be fighting."

He spun back toward Zasha. "And you ... knock it off." But his eyes, threaded through with silver in addition to the violet, making Zasha assume that's where he got his moniker, danced with amusement.

"Now sit still."

With the way he brandished the curved suturing needle at her, she obeyed, and he began sewing her up again with practiced strokes. He didn't bother with an anesthetic, and she clenched her teeth against the unpleasant sensation of a needle and thread winding through her flesh. As a cage fighter, of course it was far from the first time she'd been stitched up. It didn't stop her from wishing it'd be the last occasion for it, just as she did every time.

"I'll update Corin as soon as he gets here," Quannah said. "Which should be soon. But now, you tell us ... what happened to you? How did you end up in the Pound, and how did you end up a wolf?"

Even Kisha chilled out to listen to her tell them her story.

Zasha didn't see any advantage to keeping things from them. She didn't know anything about being a wolf, and neither would her uncles.

"I've been trained to fight my whole life," she started, and Quannah's attention didn't leave her face the entire time she spoke. "My uncles and papa, they have a gym. I earned my living fighting. Mixed martial arts in the cage, kickboxing in the ring, whatever. Anyway, that doesn't matter..."

Only, from the looks on everyone's faces, even Silver as he followed the path of the needle moving through her arm, she could tell that it did.

"My ... something bad happened ... and I was distracted, walking through the streets of Flaming Arrow, in a different neighborhood from where I lived, close to the hospital. Anyway, four dudes attacked me. No big deal. I could handle it. But then they used magic on me."

She waited while Silver tied a knot on his stitches and cut the surgical thread.

"Only one of them had magic, but I couldn't defend against it. So they took me. I could tell the guy ... Marley ... put something dark inside me, but I couldn't shake it. I passed out, and when I woke up, I was in the Pound."

Quannah's eyes flared violet again, but she didn't avoid them, losing herself to their depths as she finished.

"And by then I was a wolf. They put me in the pit with them the next day." She gestured toward Kisha and Ty with her head.

"Lie back," Silver said, pulling the boat neck of her shirt down and peering at the open wound there. "You're going to have to take your shirt off."

She hesitated for only a moment. She was a freaking *wolf*, and dark magic simmered inside her. There were far more concerning things than showing a little tit.

Silver stepped back and averted his eyes while she shed her shirt. She tossed it on the side of the bed and waited, feeling Quannah and Ty looking at her. Hell, she even felt Kisha's stare on her naked torso.

She forced herself not to move.

Silver picked up the discarded shirt, gently laid it over her breasts, then gave up worrying about her modesty, flipped it half aside, and began sewing closed the gaping wound that nearly exposed her breastbone.

"Tell us more about the dark magic," he said,

looking at what he was doing and not her face. "What did it look like? Feel like?"

She closed her eyes to the pain of the stitching and discovered herself back there, in the street the night her papa died. Her heart squeezed, though that did her no good. Her father was gone, and her uncles were probably half out of their minds searching for her.

As if the voice weren't hers, she heard herself say, "The magic was like a shadow. It looked like lightning, but dark. It crackled and arced like electricity. This Marley guy zapped me with it. And then…"

Quannah slid forward in his recliner, moving to the edge, leaning onto his elbows. "And then what?"

"And then I felt the magic tearing through me, ripping me apart. I thought I was going to die. No, that's not true. I knew they weren't trying to kill me, that they wanted me for something. I just hoped I'd die."

She hated the weakness she heard in her words. Wasn't weakness what had gotten her into this mess in the first place? If she hadn't lowered her guard, the men wouldn't have attacked her. They would have moved on to the next poor schmo who looked like an easy mark.

She snapped her eyes open and refused to meet the many eyes on her face. "It was pretty awful. I didn't know what was happening to me, but I could feel my humanity being taken from me." She shrugged off the weight of her admission and looked to Ty and Kisha. "You know the rest."

Most of it, anyway. Enough to spare her from having to recount more.

"I'm going to murder those bastards," Quannah growled into the stretching silence.

"Not without me you aren't," she said.

"Or me," Kisha said.

"Or me," Ty added.

Silver tied another knot. "I'm sure we're all ready to torch the place after what we saw there."

"We have to take out Marley and their boss guy. Both of them have magic," Zasha said. "The others I dealt with didn't."

"And by 'dealt with,'" Ty said with a wry smile, "you mean you ripped Marley's cheek off and broke a knee?"

"Yup." She smiled viciously. "I'm also hopeful I broke another guy's larynx."

Ty grinned. "See?" he told Kisha.

"See what?" she said cautiously, as if Ty were leading her into a trap.

"I told you she was one of us."

"She's not one of us."

"Her eyes say differently," Ty said, with a pointed look at Quannah.

"That's for Corin to decide when he gets here."

"Assuming the she-wolf lives that long." Kisha gave Zasha a mean-girl smile that made Zasha itch with the need to show her what she thought of bullies.

"My name isn't she-wolf," she said instead. "It's Zasha."

"Well, Zasha," Ty said. "I'm Ty."

"Yeah," she said. "I know." Obviously.

"Thanks for helping me out in there. It'd been a long three months."

She nodded, shrugging off his thanks. "I can imagine. I was glad to help. Just wish I'd gotten to have at their boss. What's his name, anyway? I'd like to put a name to the face I'm going to maul."

"We don't know," Quannah said. "But we're sure as hell going to find out."

Then, he froze.

CHAPTER NINETEEN

QUANNAH

QUANNAH WAS SURELY GOING to murder the assholes who'd forced a change on Zasha and left black magic circling around inside her, haunting her. He could see the toll it was taking, weighing down the brightness of her blue and now violet eyes, even if she tried to shrug it off. It would likely end up killing her, despite how long she'd managed to survive so far.

He was going to make every single sleazebucket responsible for taking her and the rest of their wolves pay a hefty price for their sins.

But first...

Corin.

Something wasn't right with the alpha. Quannah could feel that wrongness thrumming through his bones, like a guitar string being plucked off tune.

Quannah was the only member of their pack

who could use the pack link to communicate up the chain to the alpha. Even so, he didn't do it unless Corin was expecting him to, usually to report in after completing some task Corin had assigned him. As pack beta, Quannah might command a lot of respect from the other wolves, but he was still second in charge. Which meant his job, as much as the others, was to follow the alpha's orders.

Even so, he didn't hesitate to reach out to Corin then.

Alpha, is everything okay?

Corin was supposed to be on his way back home to the Smoky Mountains. He should be nearly arriving, which meant he'd hear his call as easily as if Quannah were standing right next to him.

Despite the churning sense of ill ease spreading to fill him, he waited, giving the shifter sufficient time to free himself of whatever he was doing to answer.

Alpha? Quannah prompted again.

When no answer was forthcoming, Quannah stood, making Silver rush to his side like he was some sort of weakling. Before the mother-hen shifter could say a word, Quannah held up a hand and focused, closing his eyes in an attempt to tap into his alpha's energy.

He'd never tried it before; it probably went

against some pack hierarchy rule. Quannah didn't care. Something was definitely wrong.

Corin! he broadcast at the alpha, but this time he also reached out to the man with his inner vision. Besides having been raised a wolf shifter his entire life, born to wolf shifter parents, his lineage was native to the continent now known as North America. Their tribe's knowledge of the supernatural extended beyond shifters. To them, all of creation was interconnected. Quannah should be able to feel Corin, despite his lack of verbal response.

But though Quannah pushed out his energy, seeking for that signature he imagined he'd be able to identify as Corin, he came up blank.

When he finally opened his eyes, everyone, including Zasha, was staring at him. Zasha was the only one who didn't look worried. She was also the only one who didn't know him.

Chenoa and Roan were moving toward him, and Ty and Kisha looked ready to bolt from their beds.

Scrawled across all their faces was the pressing question: "What's wrong?"

Before saying anything, he closed his eyes again, and once more reached for the alpha. He was sure he should be able to feel him. His mother, if she were alive, would certainly have been able to. She'd been able to feel every member of the pack as easily as if she were the alpha.

Quannah opened his eyes and met Silver's. "Is it safe for me to start moving around now?"

Silver's eyes widened and he shook his head. "No, of course not. If *any* silver is left in your system, it could still prove fatal, even at this stage of recovery."

"How big is the risk after how much of the toxin I've eliminated?"

Quannah wanted nothing more than to tear off and begin the search for his alpha. But if something had happened to Corin, their pack needed Quannah more than ever. He couldn't risk himself even if he wanted to. His responsibility was to the entire Smoky Mountain Pack.

Silver was still shaking his head, but more slowly now, as if he'd realized already what might prompt Quannah to ask questions such as these.

Silver dragged out the words: "The risk is lesser now. But it still exists. I estimate that you need at least another four days of limited movement to be completely safe."

"What's the risk now?" Quannah pressed.

Silver sighed, running a harried hand through his hair. "I'd say that if you start going about your regular activities, you'll be at a ... a twenty percent risk of accelerating the spread of whatever silver is left in your system."

He paused. When Quannah didn't say anything, he added: "Which means you'd possibly die. If the silver spreads again, there's no guarantee your system will be able to expunge it again. It will be drained from fighting to expel it the first time around."

"So twenty percent?" Quannah stared blankly out the window across from him, not seeing anything. "I can live with that." Then he paused, hearing the expression he'd used. He might or might not live with that, but one of five odds of dying was a risk he'd take. After all, there was still Flynn. He wasn't as suited to leading the pack if he or Corin were out of the picture, but he'd do.

Decision made, Quannah turned to Ty and Kisha: "You two stay and rest."

"What the hell's going on, man?" Ty asked, kicking his legs off the side of the bed despite what his beta had just told him.

"Corin is in danger."

Ty and Kisha hopped out of bed, and Roan and Chenoa looked ready to bolt out the door at a full run.

"I told you two to stay and heal," he told Ty and Kisha. "You won't be any help if you're not full strength.

"With all due respect, Quannah, that's bullshit. We're in no worse shape than you. We weren't shot with silver, and we already purged the Wolf Woofer from our systems. We're good to go."

Neither Ty nor Kisha looked ready to go—beyond the determined gleam in their eyes, glinting around violet streaks. But determination was most of the fight.

He nodded. "Fine. But pull back if you have to. Let's go."

With a few long strides, he was at the door, sweeping through it, his bare feet feeling the cold of the damp grass. Chenoa, Roan, Ty, and Kisha filed out behind him, and he turned to them.

"You can't come," he said, looking Zasha up and down. Silver had covered her stitches with large patches of gauze, but he hadn't forgotten how injured she still was—or what circulated within her.

"Save your breath," she said. "I'm coming. If you don't have to lie around following Doc's orders, neither do I. Nothing you say will change my mind, and it sounds like it's urgent, so let's get to it."

"This is pack business. Stay in the infirmary till we get back."

She crossed her arms over her chest, pushing her tits up, nipples straining at the flimsy fabric of the scrubs reminding him she still wore no bra. When he finally looked at her face, she was staring blankly at him, as if she hadn't caught him ogling—again—and as if the matter were already decided.

"You're not part of the pack," he snapped.

"Apparently my eyes say differently. And so long as I'm here, any fight is my fight."

"That's ridiculous."

"If you knew me better, you wouldn't think so."

He waggled his jaw, felt his nostrils flare, and narrowed his eyes at her.

She didn't flinch.

"Fine. Your funeral."

Then he spun on his heel, grinding it into the rich dirt, and stalked across the open field between buildings until he reached the armory.

He didn't know what was happening with Corin, but he had to prepare for the worst. And when it came to wolf shifters, the worst was the hunters, the Protectors of Humanity as the Society openly called itself in supernatural circles, touting themselves as the saviors of all saviors, overlooking the fact that they were zealots who'd lost sight of reality—murderers.

As Quannah yanked open the door to their armory, he hoped Corin had just gotten busy with some woman and didn't want to answer Quannah because he was busy getting some.

Of course that was nothing like their alpha. Not that he didn't like his women, but he'd never put anyone else above the needs of the pack, not even himself. Still, Quannah had to hope. Or maybe he was drunk off the moonshine the pack got from a neighboring tribe, which a shaman imbued with something beyond the ordinary that was capable of bypassing the wolf shifters' enhanced healing to intoxicate them—giving them time away from the burdens of living in a world where there was always a target on their backs.

Maybe Corin was just trying to forget for a while, Quannah thought, though he understood it couldn't be true. The responsibility of being an alpha would weigh on any man, but Corin had filled the role for more than a decade.

As Quannah started wrapping a gun belt around his waist, and then reached for a shoulder holster as well, he caught Zasha staring, wide-eyed, at the extent of their arsenal.

"You thought all we had were claws and teeth?" he asked on a hollow-sounding chuckle.

She shook her head, her long, dark blonde hair sliding into her face. "No. I just didn't think you'd need any of this when you have the awesome teeth and claws."

"We shouldn't need guns. But the hunters use them."

Ty was strapping on his own shoulder holster. "And they load every motherfucking thing they can get their hands on with silver."

"True." Silver strapped up too. Gone was the mother hen, he was all warrior. "And they have all those alchemical potions and tonics too."

"You sound jealous," Zasha said, tying her hair up into a knot. Her breasts strained against the fabric of her shirt as she lifted her arms, Quannah couldn't help but notice.

"I'm totally jealous," Silver told her, stuffing a Glock 19 into one of his holsters. "But I'll get there too. Someday. Then they'll be sorry they messed with us."

Hair up and out of her face, Zasha reached into the bin of holsters and grabbed one. She'd never had much need for guns, not when she trained to fight in the ring or cage, and it took her a few moments to realize the strap she'd grabbed was for her thigh. But that was even better; she grabbed a second one.

Roan eyed her. "You can't fight like that. Come with me. You look to be about my size."

Which meant small but powerful.

Roan didn't wait for Zasha to answer, and led the

way. Zasha hesitated only a moment before following her out.

The second the two of them were gone, Quannah told the others: "I don't want to alarm anyone. For all we know, Corin might be just fine. This is in case he needs our help. I want us to be ready."

Silver, Ty, Kisha, and Chenoa nodded. Chenoa was reaching for a rifle. Quannah placed a hand on her arm. "I want you to stay here."

She raised her dark eyebrows, but didn't say a word. Calm, always calm, he loved that about her.

"Seek out the elders. Tell them our alpha isn't responding to my calls. Tell them to do their magic and protect the pack."

Within the Smoky Mountain Pack, there were several members of the Katoa, including a few elders, who led their own lives as fringe members. Of the younger Katoa, only Chenoa was even tempered; the others were as volatile and fiery as comets.

Quannah didn't think the elders possessed magic the way the mages of the world wielded it. They didn't consult grimoires or spell books to cast their spells, but they wove magic of some sort just the same.

"You'll update me, then?" Chenoa asked. "As soon as you find him?"

"Of course," Quannah said, and she turned to leave.

"Chenoa?"

She glanced back.

"And tell them about Zasha. See if there's something they can do to counteract the dark magic inside her."

She nodded, shiny black hair sliding in a uniform sheet, hooked the rifle back in its slot, and left.

"What's the plan, boss?" Ty asked.

Quannah scowled at him. Ty knew he didn't like being called that ... which was why he did it.

Ty smiled tightly at him, the strain of whatever was happening to their alpha weighing on all of them.

"We go find him. And if he's in trouble, we fight until he's out of it."

"Sounds like a solid plan to me." Ty hitched a rifle over his shoulder and eyed a semi-automatic.

Nolan, Lucian, Webb, Dax, Jett, and Hayes, Quannah called out just to them, using a limited pack link. *Drop whatever you're doing, gear up at the armory, and meet us by the cars in ten. We're rollin' out.*

Then, weaponed up, Quannah walked out, Silver, Ty, and Kisha following.

"We meet by the cars in ten. If anyone asks, tell

them we're just going to meet up with Corin. Leave out the part about him not answering me."

"You got it, boss," Ty said, and the three of them went separate ways, heading toward their cabins, no doubt.

Quannah did the same. He preferred to walk barefoot, feeling the open connection to the land beneath him. Whether that was a personal preference or a tribal trait he'd inherited through the Cherokee, he didn't know. But for this he'd need boots. If they ended up in Flaming Arrow, or another equally sketchy city, no way did he want to touch anything about it more than necessary.

On his way to his cabin, he reached out to Flynn. *Meet me at my place. We need to talk.*

Flynn arrived at Quannah's seconds after he did.

"I was nearby," Flynn said by way of greeting as his attention skimmed across Quannah and his weapons. "It looks like we do need to talk."

Leaving the door open so Flynn could follow him around as he grabbed boots, a belt, a couple of his favorite personal blades, and a hair tie, he sat to pull on his boots. He had the first on when he kicked it off and decided on his moccasins instead. He might need stealth; he'd stuff his boots in the trunk.

"Corin was supposed to be back by now, and he isn't answering me."

Flynn sat heavily into the single hardback chair next to the small writing table by the window. "Fuck."

"I don't know that anything's wrong. Maybe we'll get lucky and we'll just find him with his pants around his ankles."

"Yeah." But Flynn sounded about as convinced as Quannah was. "You think it's the hunters or the Pound?"

Moccasins on, Quannah glanced up at him. "No idea. Let's just hope it's not both, or we'll be battling magic, and different kinds on all sides."

Flynn stood. "I'll gear up."

Quannah rose too, weaving the sheaths for his knives through his belt. "No. I need you here, for now anyway. We still don't know if anything's wrong. But be ready to go, and choose about a dozen of the best to come with you. I'm taking most of the crew I went into the Pound with."

"You got it. You let me know and we'll be ready to leave in five."

"Great, and Flynn...?"

Flynn stopped halfway out the door.

"Be ready for anything. Corin has never not answered me before."

With a tight nod and tighter shoulders, the gamma of the pack stalked out the door. Not only would he get a troop of fighters ready, he'd have the entire pack on alert, hopefully without freaking anyone out.

With a minute to spare, Quannah arrived at the cars. Roan and Zasha were there too. Zasha wore tight, stretchy jeans that allowed for movement, a tight top that left none of her contours to the imagination, and light fighting boots. The stark white of her patches of gauze stood out against the guns she had strapped to her.

"Where'd you get those?" she asked, pointing at Quannah's blades. "They look wicked."

"They are." He grinned despite himself. Instead of checking him out, she was scoping out his weapons.

"Hayes, Ro, and Zasha, you're with me," Quannah said. "The rest of you, divide up. A driver plus two or three per car. We want to be fast and able to split up if we have to. Corin was traveling back to us from the west, which means he probably went through Flaming Arrow. We have to find him. Be ready for anything. We'll head out of here in opposite directions, doing what we usually do in case of surveillance. Once you're sure you've lost any possible tails, we'll meet up at the overlook of Black Bear Ridge. Any questions?"

"Do we know if anything's happened to Corin?" Webb asked.

"All we know is that he hasn't answered me." He pursed his lips before adding: "And a bad feeling in my gut."

Nolan whistled under his breath. "Damn. We'd better get moving, then."

Quannah nodded, got in the driver's seat of his Jeep Wrangler Unlimited, and revved the engine.

Roan and Hayes hopped in the back, so Zasha took the passenger seat. He looked over at her.

"What?" she said. "Shotgun was open."

She was brassy, this one.

She laid a shotgun across her lap, cracked open and pointing toward the floor.

"Well? Watcha waitin' for?"

He had no idea. He peeled out of the parking lot, tossing over his shoulder: "Ro, you watch Zasha."

Sure, he did genuinely need Roan to keep an eye on the she-wolf. She was unpredictable, had volatile black magic rolling through her, was injured, and overall was an unknown entity.

But that's not why he said it like that, and he knew it.

"What do you mean, she's supposed to 'watch' me?" Zasha snapped right away, turning in her seat to glare at him. "I'm not some fucking TV screen."

"No, but you're not part of this pack and you were made by black magic."

"Enough fucking said," Hayes grumbled from the back seat.

"No matter what your eyes say," Quannah added anyway.

"Wait," Hayes said. "Her eyes? Don't tell me that..."

"Yup," Roan said happily, which made Quannah suspicious. Roan was a live wire who almost always liked to get into trouble.

"But," Hayes said.

Roan again replied: "Yeppers."

Hayes whistled under his breath. "But how?"

"No idea," Quannah said. "But her eyes have the pack violet in them, no doubt."

"Could Corin have inducted her while he was away somehow?" Hayes asked.

"Don't see how, but it's the only way for a wolf to join us." Even so, Quannah suspected Zasha broke the rules. He just didn't know which ones yet.

"Why don't we just focus on getting back so we can ask?" she said.

Quannah tore down a gravel road and glanced at her. "You're sure you're up for a fight?"

She scowled at him in reply, then stared out the windshield.

Roan chuckled—again happily. "She's ready all right."

"But this isn't even her fight," Hayes said, his forehead still scrunched as he tried to figure the she-wolf out.

"Any fight that gets me answers and closer to getting out of this mess is my fight," Zasha said. "And the sooner I get to leave, the better." Then her voice softened. "I have people looking for me."

Quannah didn't have the heart to tell her that whatever people they were, they wouldn't want her now that she was a shifter. The humans never did.

He focused on the road, picking up speed even more, and pushed his energy out to find the alpha.

He came back empty, and floored it.

CHAPTER TWENTY

GIDEON

GIDEON BIT his bottom lip to keep his mouth from spreading into the grin that was fighting to break free. He wasn't used to holding back smiles, as he rarely had reason for them, but an attack team rode in the van with him. He must maintain professional indifference.

Even so, one side of his mouth tilted up slightly.

His superiors had been pleased with him when he told them he'd discovered the location of the Smoky Mountain Pack. Gideon set up a conference call with them, a risk since the three men and two women who ran the Society behind the scenes didn't like to be disturbed—and knew how to express their displeasure in the most expedient and severe of ways. If the Five, as Gideon called them, didn't sufficiently appreciate his news, he'd be demoted, and he'd worked too hard and dedicated too much of himself to this organization to go anywhere but up. He had to get credit for finding the Smoky Mountain Pack, and if he didn't go straight to the top with the news, he suspected Mister Blome, his direct supervisor, would claim the discovery as his own. Gideon had never liked him. His eyes were shifty, never making eye contact for more than a few seconds at a time, and he dressed too impeccably.

Gideon's armpits dampened as a secretary connected his call to each of the Five. But he knew they'd like what he had to say, and he'd been right.

After ordering him to assemble the strongest team he could, they commented among each other that perhaps it was time to consider Gideon for a promotion. That perhaps he could replace Mister Blome, or rise above him.

Gideon hadn't said a word while he listened, barely daring to breathe into the receiver on his end. The Five had made no promises, but decisions came down unexpectedly, and Gideon wouldn't be surprised if he were promoted sooner rather than later.

Now that he had the alpha of the pack, he was betting it would happen within the month. Very few hunters had ever captured an alpha. Even fewer had ever sequestered the alpha of a pack as large as this one. Those who had were legends among them.

Sitting in the back of the van along a bench, he stretched out his legs and looked toward the locked back door, allowing his smile to pop free while no one could see him.

He couldn't believe his luck! He hadn't felt this lucky since Amalie swept into his life. Quickly, before the familiar grief could rush in, he pushed away thoughts of Amalie before even alighting on a single memory of her brilliant smile. He, Gideon Slate, had done what no one else had ever managed to do, and he had done it all on his own.

On a final reconnaissance mission to scout out the best avenues of attack, Gideon had been driving out of the Smoky Mountain Pack area, which covered hundreds of acres, when he'd passed a small, rural gas station. He didn't need to stop for gas yet, but something led him to pull in at the station anyway, lining up next to one of two pumps. The second one was occupied, and when Gideon glanced at the man pumping gas, he swore he stopped breathing.

The man was fit and strong, as most of the monsters were, looking human to anyone who didn't know better. But there was a feralness to the man that Gideon wouldn't miss, not after sensing it so many times in people who then morphed into the beasts of nightmares.

Gideon took in the straight, pale blond hair and the barely there birthmark along one cheek that was the size of a silver dollar and knew he'd found Corin Shaw.

The elusive alpha of the Smoky Mountain Pack.

When Corin looked up at him, Gideon had nearly panicked, but he'd pulled off a convincing smile at the last moment. "Hey," he said, as if he spoke to wolf alphas every day. "How's it goin'?"

Corin stared at him for a beat too long before nodding a hello.

Corin was suspicious of him. Either that, or he was always wary of people he didn't know. Gideon's mind went blank for a few horrifying seconds he couldn't spare while he realized that this was his chance and he had no idea how to capitalize on it.

He went through the motions of unscrewing his gas cap and swiping his credit card. When he slid the nozzle into his tank, the lever popped on Corin's pump, announcing it full.

Gideon didn't have time for a good plan, and Corin knew something was up. The alpha wasn't taking his eyes off him, careful to move so that his back was never turned as he replaced the nozzle on the fuel pump and screwed on his gas cap.

It was then or never.

Gideon pretended to be putting his wallet in his Ford pickup and grabbed the Glock 26 he kept in a specially fitted holster in the door panel. It wasn't big, but it was loaded with silver bullets.

Corin was reaching a leg into the driver's side of his car when Gideon popped off three consecutive shots, hitting the alpha square in the back. He couldn't afford for him to get away, but he also couldn't kill him. The Five would want him alive, and if he wanted his promotion, he had to do what the Five wanted.

Corin fell into his open car door, but still managed to slide into his seat.

Gideon reached into his truck again and emerged with an extendable, electrified prod. Even on the wolves, they worked well with the amount of wattage each jolt gave.

Gideon raced toward the alpha, who was attempting to fit his key in the ignition, and he kept missing. The silver bullets were starting to do their job. They should have taken him down entirely, but to be an alpha of a large pack, Corin had to be strong.

Gideon jammed the prod against his arm, bare beneath a t-shirt sleeve, and zapped him. The wolf's body went tight, and blood spurted out of the three bullet holes in his back. Gideon noticed no exit wounds through the front of his chest, which was good. The bullets had to remain inside for the silver to weaken him.

For good measure, Gideon clicked the prod on again, pressing it to Corin's neck this time. Once the alpha slumped over the steering wheel, his breathing shallow, Gideon ran back to his truck and yanked a vial of Wolf Woofer from a Velcro holder along the driver's side door—one of several in the car. Though the street drug was usually taken orally, the Society lab distilled the drug into a liquid that all Gideon had to do was pour onto the alpha's skin, where it would absorb and allow Gideon to avoid being bitten when he was trying to otherwise force the drug down a wolf's throat. The skin directed the Wolf Woofer straight into the bloodstream.

This was the kind of thing that made the Society great. Teams of scientists supported the hunters. Researchers and aides in all sorts of fields worked to make them more effective at what they did best.

At what Gideon did best.

He upended the vial on Corin's slumped head, tangling the liquid in his hair so it would tarry in running off, and once it did, it would drip down his body.

The unmistakable pumping of a shotgun froze Gideon in place.

"What the hell's goin' on here?" a thick drawl demanded.

Gideon put his hands up, still holding the vial and prod, and turned slowly, moving to lean against the back panel of the alpha's car as he did so. Corin should be out and unable to attack. But Gideon had hunted the monsters long enough to understand that assumptions could be as fatal as their bite. He felt safer with a car pressed against him.

"I'm an undercover police detective," Gideon said, repeating the story every hunter used while out on the job. "This is an extremely dangerous wanted fugitive."

The man, who appeared to be in his early seventies without an ounce of brittleness about him, took a few steps forward to peer into Corin's car.

"D'ya kill 'im?"

"No, he's just out. I've sedated him, but I dosed him only enough to buy me time to get him to the station. I need to hurry."

"Don't look to me like he's goin' nowhere anytime soon."

"You'd be surprised at how resilient he is." Gideon snuck a glance back at Corin; he was out cold—for now. The Wolf Woofer should be working quickly to disarm his ability to communicate with the rest of his pack, because yes, the Society had discovered that the beasts could speak to each other in some way—telepathy or something. It was dangerous and unholy.

Gideon had to hurry. If Corin managed to get a message off, the rest of his pack would soon descend on them. Gideon was counting on the speed with which he'd attacked, and the amount of assaults he'd thrown at him.

Hands still up, Gideon forced his face into a friendly mask. He scrunched his forehead in obvious concern. "This guy's really dangerous, and he runs with a gang that's as dangerous as he is. I need to get out of here with him before they can come looking for him."

Inside, Gideon congratulated himself for his fast thinking. This wasn't part of the spiel the Society coached him to use.

"My badge is in my truck. Let me get it to show you."

The man scowled fiercely, but finally nodded, jerking his shotgun in the direction of Gideon's truck. "Any funny business and I'll shoot first." He didn't add on that he'd add questions later. From the hardened tilt of his eyes, he wasn't asking questions. He'd call the real police and let them deal with things.

Moving as if the gas station owner were a viper preparing to strike, Gideon walked to his truck.

"I'm going to put what I have in my hand down to get my badge. Don't shoot."

"Don't give me reason to and I won't."

Gideon laid the empty vial and prod on his seat, and lowered his visor. His fake badge, which looked as real as any true police badge thanks to the Society's connections, was hooked to it.

"I have my badge," Gideon said, beginning to feel the itch to get the alpha out of there before anything could go wrong. "I'm going to turn back around slowly."

When Gideon finally pointed his badge at the man, he inched closer, not moving the barrel of the shotgun, which still trained on Gideon's chest.

"Looks real 'nough," the man finally said, his voice like raw gasoline.

"You can call and ask for my supervisor to confirm." His cover would check out. The Society didn't leave details to chance.

"No need."

"Would you mind lowering your gun, then?" Gideon asked.

"I would. I seen 'nough Bond movies to know how fast things can go sideways."

"Well, I have to get him out of here before he wakes up. Will you help me get him into my truck?"

The man scowled long and hard, deep grooves

etching into his forehead, jowls, and eyes. "I suppose."

Finally, he lowered his gun.

Gideon took that as a sign that he could hustle. However, he still updated the man as he moved so he wouldn't be surprised by anything.

Gideon removed the gas nozzle from his tank and positioned his truck sideways behind Corin's car, trying to cut the distance they'd have to move him as much as possible.

The shotgun man was as strong as he looked, wiry and muscly despite age, and once he put down his gun, he was able to help Gideon drag Corin into his truck and plop him on the bench seat. Gideon didn't even care that the alpha was getting blood on his refurbished upholstery. After his promotion, he'd be able to get as many trucks like this one as he wanted.

When Gideon finished moving Corin's car around back and tossed the shotgun man the keys in case he had to move it, the man said: "You know you ain't supposed to shoot guns in a gas station, right?"

Gideon couldn't be sure, but he thought the old man's eyes might be twinkling. After all, he'd been willing to do the same thing.

Gideon shrugged with a tentative smile. "Trust me, if you knew how bad this guy is, you would've done it too. I'll send someone to square things with you as soon as I can."

The Society took care of people and situations. The old man would probably be paid for his assistance, and thus be well-disposed to help again someday.

Gideon managed to get out of there before Corin could rouse, and before anyone from his pack could arrive to assist him.

As soon as he was out of sight of the gas station, he pulled over and dosed the alpha with even more Wolf Woofer. He had no idea what the wolf was capable of, and he didn't want to risk it.

But by the time he got the alpha to the warehouse where his assault team was assembling to invade the Smoky Mountain Pack, the alpha's breathing was shallow and raspy.

Panicked that the alpha might die, Gideon changed plans. The team loaded the alpha into the back of the van and they squealed out of there, heading for one of the Society's medical facilities.

After shackling the alpha's ankles and hands with silver cuffs, the medic on the team had hooked him up to fluids that looked like an IV bag, but Gideon knew wasn't. The medic would be trying to counteract the silver just enough to keep the alpha alive. And just as Gideon was good at his job, so would be the medic.

Gideon relaxed into the back of the van—as much as he ever relaxed anyway—and leaned his head against the cold steel behind him. The alpha was his. He was an even greater prize than the beta Gideon had been planning on capturing. Now that he knew where the pack lived, he could swarm the place later. With their alpha missing, it was unlikely they'd move a pack so numerous. They'd be searching for the alpha instead. Gideon had the feeling he had time.

He'd claim all the prizes.

One at a time.

Secure in the sight of the alpha unconscious and shackled both to limit movement and to the stretcher he was on, he closed his eyes for a few minutes, allowing himself to think of Amalie and how proud she'd be of him.

For you, Amalie. So they can't do to anyone else what they did to you.

Finally, Gideon allowed himself to smile.

CHAPTER TWENTY-ONE

ZASHA

THEY MOSTLY RODE in silence while Quannah wove through circuitous routes, driving fast and barely slowing to take turns. Three other cars pulled out of the parking lot at the pack's home, which, from what Zasha could tell at a glance, consisted of a whole lot of cabins and some larger buildings that she assumed were communal. The three cars had quickly veered off in different directions, proving to Zasha that this pack took its secrecy seriously.

She'd never felt safe while living in Flaming Arrow, but she hadn't felt hunted either, as they clearly did. As she perhaps should now that she was something new, different, and terrifying.

In the back seat, Roan and Hayes looked constantly out the windows—front, side, and back—

keeping watch for a threat that could come from any direction.

Beside her, Quannah's body carried a controlled tension. He was ready for anything at any moment, making her experience a rushing tingle that swept through her entire body. This sensation, at least, was familiar. It was the same she felt before entering the ring to fight. She was grateful for it and the knowledge that, though she might be so different in some ways, she remained the same in other ways. She was a fighter, always had been, always would be. No matter what else she was, she could do this. She could fight her way to answers and safety. Maybe, if she was lucky, she could even fight her way to a semblance of normalcy, though she had no idea what that might look like now.

When Quannah took a sharp right turn onto a paved street and then pulled the Jeep into an open lot to skid to a stop, she looked at him.

"The overlook to Black Bear Ridge," he said. "The others will be here soon."

Without additional comment, Quannah, Roan, and Hayes got out of the car, so she followed suit. Beyond the small parking pull-off, verdant mountains spread as far as the eye could see. Under other circumstances, the view would be stunning, worthy of an overlook status. But all she could do was search for threats, scanning the mountains below them for any moving points or trails of dust that would suggest approaching cars.

But few cars drove in any direction, and none felt particularly threatening, though she wasn't sure she would know if they were.

"What do you smell?" Quannah asked Hayes, drawing her attention back to the shifter who'd been so ready to shoot her in the head at the Pound.

Hayes was shaking his head, shabby haircut bouncing with the movement. "He hasn't been here recently. I scent him, but nothing that will help us. There's no trail out of here."

Quannah nodded solemnly, staring out over the outlook as she had. She wondered what he saw; she didn't think he was taking in the view either.

"Can't all of you smell things?" Zasha asked. "I mean, better than most people? I can smell things I couldn't before."

Quannah's gaze remained on the stretch of mountains in front of them. "We can, but Hayes can scent better than most."

"Yeah, he's got a super sniffer," Roan said with a chuckle.

Zasha was learning that the petite redhead was more likely to smile than the rest of them.

Quannah stood at the edge of the asphalt, his

bearing strong, regal. Zasha couldn't help but be drawn to him, even as she hoped she'd find the way out of there, away from the pack—and away from him.

A head taller than she was, his forearm muscles and biceps bulged with his readiness to take down their as-yet-invisible enemy. His stance emanated strength and speed, and she had no doubt he could tear off at a full sprint and outrun almost anybody. She suspected even she'd have to work to keep up with him in those light moccasins, and she was fast, faster than anyone else she knew in her previous life. On his person, he wore only a few handguns and those two long, sharp blades that she wanted to touch. She itched with the desire to reach out to him and run her fingers along those ... blades. Yeah, it was just the knives she wanted. Though she had no use for them inside the cage or the ring, she loved blades. Daggers, swords, knives—anything sharp and shiny was her thing.

He'd pulled his straight, black, shiny hair into a tight ponytail that rested against the nape of his neck, exposing every angle of his face to her examination. His nose was long and sharp at the tip, his mouth broad, and his skin the color of her own if she sunned all summer long. He clearly was of indigenous descent, his eyes dark, intense, and carrying the responsibility of honoring the ways of a people who understood this world better than most.

His stare was so intent that she imagined he was lost to his thoughts, not even seeing the mountains rolling outward before him.

"I don't know if we'll have to fight, but you really shouldn't with those big gashes."

His tone suggested that he cared.

"You'll be a liability. You'll slow us down."

She frowned. "I haven't been a liability to anyone in my entire life." Maybe she had been when she was little, before her mother left and she required more care. But she'd been fending for herself and her papa for as long as she could remember. She started cooking meals for him the day after her mother left. She'd been seven. "You worry about yourself and let me worry about me."

"Don't worry, Quannah," Roan piped up from where she and Hayes paced on the other side of the car. "I'll keep an eye out for her."

Zasha whirled to face the ginger. "I don't need anyone to watch me."

Roan took a few steps toward her on her short legs, bringing her hands to her waist. "How long have you been a wolf? How much do you know about wolves and how we work? What we're capable of and what we aren't?"

Zasha didn't reply. There was no need.

"How much do you know about dark magic?" the redhead persisted, with a healthy dose of the stereotypical fire. "How self-aware do you think you'd be if black magic were making you act in unusual ways, if it were controlling you?"

Roan smirked, knowing she had Zasha.

"And that's why I'm going to look out for you." She ran a hand through shoulder-length hair as red as maple leaves when they turn in autumn. "And also because I have the feeling you kick ass, and I can't wait to see that. There aren't enough of us fiery women in this pack."

"There're too fucking many," Hayes grumbled, and Quannah laughed, a dry sound, like he didn't laugh often enough.

The beta wanted her gone as much as she wanted to be gone.

Over the next several minutes, the three other cars pulled in next to them. Quannah checked in with all of them. No one had seen or smelled anything that would help them find the alpha.

"We split up," Quannah said to the group of them as they stood in a rough line in front of the view. "You guys head toward Knobby Hollow," he told Lucian, Nolan, and Silver. "You go in the Bloody Basin direction," he told Webb, Dax, and Ty. "And you, to Lowlands," he said to Kisha and Jett. "We'll check out Flaming Arrow."

"You got it," Jett said, and others responded in kind.

"You all have charged cells, yes?"

Nods.

"I don't want the drivers making the calls. Register who's not driving, and call them. Keep everyone in the loop. You smell or see something odd, you call. You check out a place and see nothing, you call. When you're ready to move on to someplace else, you call my car and I'll tell you where to go."

More nods.

"I still haven't heard from Corin. At this point, we're going to operate as if someone's done something to him or taken him. By now, he should've checked in with me. Be on full alert. If someone's messed with our alpha, and they understand who they have, they'll know we're coming for him. It's probably hunters, but it could be the Pound too."

"Or some other trigger-happy morons who think just because we turn into wolves means we have no common sense or decency." This was Nolan, and he sounded bitter. Zasha was starting to think he had reason to be, and she'd grown up around people who believed werewolves to be vicious monsters. Hell, did she still think that? Was that what she really was? What they were? What Quannah was?

Quannah scanned the group, looking at each of them. "Stay sharp. Stay alive. Kill only if you need to."

Hayes cracked his knuckles and his neck. Quannah pointed at him. "No shooting unless it's the only way."

Then the beta took in the rest of them. "But if it's your lives or theirs, don't hesitate."

"You got it, boss," Ty said, and then everyone dispersed. In no more than a minute, everyone was loaded into their cars and pulling out.

Quannah went last, idling until he'd given the other two cars enough of a head start that their trajectories wouldn't necessarily seem tied if someone were watching the exit of the road around the bend, out of sight of the overlook.

Facing her, Quannah's eyes were dark and stormy as he said: "We can withstand a lot of abuse. We'll eventually heal from almost anything so long as we still have our hearts and our heads."

Zasha swallowed. That was some intense shit right there.

"But if you get nicked by anything with silver, those rules go out the window. If you get hit with silver, you need to let someone know right away."

She nodded, serious as a heart attack, and she knew full well how quickly those could kill. "Got it. But I don't have a cell to let anyone know."

"You won't need one. I'm not letting you out of my sight."

"I thought Roan was the one watching me."

He growled, making her wonder what she said wrong, slammed the Jeep into reverse, and pulled out with more violence than was necessary.

And men say women are confusing…

While Quannah drove away from the overlook and took a hard left from the road onto a two-lane highway, her stitches started itching. She squirmed in her seat, willing the uncomfortable sensation away. It was enough to be distracting, and if they encountered someone willing to lop off heads and carve out hearts, she couldn't afford any distraction at all.

She picked at the tape holding the bandage on her arm in place.

"Don't mess with it," Roan said. "You need to keep the wound protected and clean."

Zasha continued until she peeled up the corner slightly. "I just need to look."

And once she did, her mouth dropped open. She pulled the tape all the way up, taking a swath of her fine arm hairs with it.

"What the…?"

Roan and Hayes scooted forward to look at her arm from between the front seats, and Quannah glanced at her as he drove.

She tore the bandage all the way off, brushing pieces of dark thread off her skin and onto the inside of the bandage.

"Well, I guess her wolf healing's kicked in," Hayes said.

Zasha finished sweeping the fragments of thread her body had pushed out into the bandage, rolled it into a ball, and sealed it with the tape so the stitches wouldn't fall out into Quannah's Jeep. Then she stuffed it into the side of her door, mostly because she was struggling to grasp the fact that her skin, which had been mauled to bits, was fully smooth, and pink like a newly healed injury, not so much as a fingertip's worth of open flesh exposed anymore.

This would come in handy with cage fighting or the ring, where she almost always got at least a cut or two.

"You should've left the bandage on to protect the new skin," Roan said, but she didn't sound like she expected Zasha to listen.

"I'll fight better without anything sticking to me." Zasha was already peeling back the tape around her chest wound, face pointed straight down while she worked until she revealed another patch of brand-new pink skin. She sat back. "Wow. This shit's amazing."

Quannah tilted his gaze in her direction long enough for her to want to snap at him to watch the road. But when he did return his attention to the open path in front of them, she was left wondering what his eyes had said—they'd seemed to speak volumes, and she hadn't understood a word.

"Looks like her body's accepting the dark magic," Hayes said.

Roan sank back against the back seat. "It really does."

Quannah offered a brief grunt that didn't tell Zasha anything.

"Yeah," Hayes said, apparently interpreting mangrunt. "We'll have to wait and see. Nobody survives black magic. No wolves are supposed to be made that way for a reason."

Zasha stared out the side window. "I'm not like everybody else."

"That," Quannah said while his eyes remained fixed on the road, "has been obvious from the start."

Then Hayes rolled down the window and stuck his head out like a dog, sniffing loudly.

They drove in silence for perhaps twenty minutes before Hayes whipped his head back inside the car, hair standing in all directions, and said: "I smell him! Floor it."

And floor it Quannah did. The Jeep lurched forward, sailing down the open road like the devil himself was nipping at their bumper.

CHAPTER TWENTY-TWO

QUANNAH

HE DROVE like every second mattered to his alpha, and he feared that each one did. Even without Hayes scenting Corin's trail, he suspected he would have turned in this direction anyway. That sense that something was wrong and that Corin needed them pounded through Quannah's bloodstream as insistently as the silver toxin had during the last several days.

Corin never needed *them*. As the alpha, every member of the Smoky Mountain Pack needed *him*. A wolf pack could only ever be as strong as its leader.

Quannah flew down a paved country road, along which businesses and houses—mostly worn-down and neglected—cropped up every mile or so.

Hayes yanked his head back through the open

window. "Wait! The scent's getting weaker. We gotta head back."

Quannah didn't even come to a stop, arcing the steering wheel, riding onto the shoulder, and whipping around in a wide U-turn.

Once they were heading in the right direction, he asked Hayes: "What else do you smell?"

Hayes hesitated long enough that Quannah flicked a glance at him in the rearview mirror.

"It's not clear."

Quannah tilted his lips down into a "come-on..."

Hayes looked out toward the window, but didn't stick his head out of it again yet. "Fine. It's blood, Corin's blood."

Quannah rolled his neck, trying to release some of the tension building up. "Can you tell how much?"

"No."

"It's enough that I can smell it too," Roan said.

Quannah pressed down harder on the accelerator. They whipped past a posted fifty-five mph speed limit sign at ninety miles per hour.

Zasha didn't even appear to notice. Instead, she busied herself checking the several firearms attached to her person, making sure everything was as it should be.

They blew by a small gas station that looked like it might be out of business.

"Too fast," Hayes said, and Quannah eased off the accelerator. "There. I think he might be there."

Quannah's brow furrowed. "At that gas station? It looks closed."

But he was already taking another U-turn, slower this time.

They rolled up to the gas station at a prudent sixty miles an hour.

"Pull in," Hayes said, but by then Quannah was already doing it. He smelled Corin too, and he definitely scented his blood with its unique tangy scent that was unlike anyone else's. To a wolf shifter, blood was as specific an identifier as a fingerprint.

Quannah brought the Jeep to a stop at the edge of the gas station's parking lot, leaning to look through the windshield at two outdated fuel pumps and a store that looked as if it were closed for good, but upon closer inspection wasn't. Dim lights were on inside the building that was too small to house public restrooms.

"Why would Corin stop here?" Roan asked, voicing his thought.

The alpha got down and dirty when necessary, but when he didn't, he appreciated the basic luxuries of life. Corin was more likely to drive by a gas station like this one in favor of a more modernized locale with nicer amenities. Corin always planned ahead, and he knew this area as well as Quannah did, which meant it was unlikely the alpha would have been surprised by an empty gas tank.

"It doesn't seem like Corin would stop here," Quannah finally said, but clearly he had. He opened his door. "Hayes, with me. Roan, you stay here with Zasha."

Every one of Quannah's senses prickled with alertness as Hayes drew up at his side, sniffing the air.

"Damn, this gas smells bad," he said.

But Quannah was able to pick out scents beyond the gasoline fumes, which meant the wolf with the keen sense of smell would also realize that here, in this rundown gas station in the middle of nowhere, their alpha had bled.

Quannah stalked toward the pumps, several dark stains against the old asphalt jumping out at him as if they glowed. He stared.

Hayes drew to his side. "I'd hoped I was wrong."

But Hayes' sniffer was never wrong. He was as effective as a bloodhound. The pack had tested his abilities once. He was able to follow a scent trail for more than a hundred miles.

Quannah didn't tell Hayes what to do next. The wolf knew and set about scenting the area surrounding the droplets of blood, which looked black against the tarmac now that they'd dried.

While Hayes sniffed the air, Quannah walked around to the back of the gas station.

And spotted Corin's cherry black '68 Mustang Fastback GT. He'd never abandon the car he'd refurbished himself. It was second in importance to him only to the pack. He'd named the car *Kitten*, though he called it *Kitty*, saying it purred just right.

Quannah steeled himself for the inevitable and reached out to the gamma, limiting the pack link so only Flynn could hear him. *We found Corin's car and his blood. Prepare the entire pack for a fight. And shore up the defenses there too, just in case. I'll update once I know more.*

He wasn't supposed to hear a response from anyone beyond Corin, so he didn't wait for one, approaching the Mustang to take a look inside it. His stomach tightened uncomfortably as he prayed he wouldn't find any more blood.

Crouching over, he peered inside the car and stilled, feeling his heartbeat pick up. Mindfully, he worked to slow it down. He didn't need Silver barking at him to remember that he had to take it easy so the toxin wouldn't have a chance at spreading further inside him. Now more than ever, he needed to be strong.

He straightened and pulled in deep, steadying breaths, and only once his pulse had slowed again did he pull open the door.

Unlocked.

Corin never left Kitty unprotected, and he especially wouldn't park her at a gas station like this.

Corin! Quannah tried again, but he felt his call bounce back toward him like a busy signal on a landline. Corin hadn't even heard him; he could feel it, his message floating unreceived.

He ran fingers along the handle of his favorite blade without hardly noticing. "Dammit," he grumbled aloud. "Corin, where the hell are you?"

The unmistakable *chuck-chick* of a shotgun ratcheting behind him brought his hands up in the air. It was an automatic response. He'd seen it happen too many times over the years: someone with an itchy trigger finger and a case of the misunderstandings.

"I mean no harm," Quannah called out since he was so clearly armed.

"Whatchyou doin' back here? This is private property." The man's voice was raspy but strong. Quannah had no doubt the man would shoot if Quannah gave him reason to.

"I'm looking for my friend. I didn't realize this

was private property back here. I thought it was part of the gas station, open to customers."

The man's voice drew closer. "Are you a customer?"

"I could be. I'm going to turn around to face you. I'll keep my hands up in the air so you can see them the whole time, okay?"

"Okay."

Even without looking, Quannah could tell the shotgun's double barrels were pointed at his back. Once he turned, he confirmed it. He started to ease his hands down, talking as he did so.

"This car belongs to a friend of mine. Have you seen him? I think he's hurt."

"Keep those hands up." The man, in his early seventies but not letting the years slow him down, traced the path he wanted Quannah's hands to take with the gun.

Quannah pushed them back up. "Come on."

"You got more weapons than an NRA parade. You keep them hands up till I tell ya otherwise."

"My friend..." Quannah said. "Have you seen him? He's blond, about my height, bright blue eyes."

"Yeah, I seen 'im."

Quannah schooled himself not to react as Zasha appeared from around the back of the gas station, rounding the store from the other side. The man hadn't seen her.

"Where is he now?" Quannah asked, eyes trained on the man, not his shotgun. A gun was only dangerous because of the person on the other end of it. At least the man's eyes were steady—as were his hands. He looked as comfortable with a gun in them as Quannah was.

"The cops took him."

"The cops?" Quannah drew his brows low. That made no sense. Corin didn't do anything to draw attention to himself once he was outside the pack's boundaries. It was one of the main rules of the Smoky Mountain Pack, and it was Corin's mandate that they operate beyond view of the hunters' radar.

"What kind of cops?" Quannah asked, watching Zasha draw closer, silent as a wolf on padded paws in Roan's light combat boots, which wasn't easy. "Local police? State? Sheriff's office?"

The man hesitated. "Don't know. Think the badge was state. Or maybe a Fed."

"Maybe a Fed?" Quannah shook his head. "My friend wouldn't have done anything to be taken by any police. I think he was kidnapped."

The man shook his head; the shotgun remained steady. "No, it was a cop, and your friend done something he shouldn't've."

Zasha moved directly behind him, within striking distance, and the man still hadn't heard her approach. The she-wolf was *good*. Quannah and no more than another handful of wolves in their entire pack were capable of that kind of stealth.

He felt her stare on his face but didn't meet it. She wouldn't expect him to. She knew he was a trained warrior; she obviously was too, which meant they spoke the same language. The heat of her stare on his face was her signal to him to be ready to move in case the old guy got a shot off while she was overpowering him.

He counted off in his head. *One. Two. Three.*

Then he leapt to the side at precisely the same moment as Zasha rounded the man, slammed a hand under the barrel of the gun, and knocked it upward.

The shotgun boomed off a shot, but it went high, disappearing into the clear sky overhead and hurting nothing.

In seconds, Zasha gripped the shotgun, used the stock to sweep the man's legs out from under him, and stretched out an arm to soften his fall. The moment he was down, she rolled him over, straddled his waist, and pinned his arms behind him.

He stretched his neck back so his face wouldn't press against the aged asphalt.

Damn, she was good. Roan or Kisha couldn't

have done it any faster, and they were the pack's best female fighters.

The man restrained, Zasha looked back at Quannah, waiting.

The beta wiped the surprise from his face and walked over to them, crouching in front of the man.

Roan and Hayes joined them, and Hayes whispered to Quannah: "The trail ends there. He was taken out of here. He's gone."

"Don't hurt me," the man said in a voice that was now far less fierce than it had been two minutes ago.

Quannah moved around in front of him so the man could look up at him, though the beta didn't think he had a clear view of him at that angle. But he wasn't about to tell Zasha to ease up. She wasn't hurting him. And besides, it was hot as hell to see her like this. Her hair, pulled away from her face, allowed him to take all of her in. Muscles tight and ready, her eyes with those perplexing violet streaks were focused, ready for the fight to continue.

She looked back at him, but he let his gaze dip down across her body anyway. The way she was straddling the other man made Quannah think of whom he'd rather she be straddling...

Her eyebrows rose in question.

He smiled, couldn't help himself. Yeah. He'd

have to find the way to get her to practice those moves on him. *Naked*.

Then he looked down at the man again, his shotgun abandoned next to them on the ground.

"I *told* you I wasn't going to hurt you but you didn't listen." Quannah didn't blame the man for not believing him, as he didn't figure he would've believed a stranger who looked like him either.

"Lemme go."

"Sure we will. Just as soon as you tell us what happened to our friend." Quannah didn't enjoy threats or violence, but a beta had to do for his pack what he had to do.

"I told you. It was cops."

"Yeah, and I heard you. Now try again."

The man wiggled his shoulders and strained against the tight hold Zasha maintained on his forearms. "She's hurting me."

"Then you'd better talk fast."

Zasha put more pressure on his arms, straining his shoulders, which clearly weren't all that flexible since the angle at which Zasha pulled them wasn't that severe.

But he hissed in evident discomfort. "It was a cop, I swear to ya."

"No cop would be looking for our friend."

"Well, he showed me a badge an' everything. Said your friend was a wanted fugitive."

"Then he lied."

"It's seeming like, I'd guess."

"There's no guessing. He lied. He took our friend against his will, and now we need to find him. And you're going to help us do that. Tell me everything you know."

"I don't know nothin', I swear to ya."

Zasha pulled on his arms some more, leaning over his back. Her breasts swelled over the low cut of Roan's shirt and Quannah looked. It was a *nice* sight.

"Fine, fine," the man said, drawing the beta's attention back to him. "I'll tell you everything I know, but it ain't much."

"Start talking," Zasha said, "and we'll tell you when it's enough."

It was like she was made for this, and she was supposed to be overcome by black magic, not operating as well as any of their pack members, trained to battle the hunters since they could walk.

"All I know is your friend pulled up in that sweet 'Stang," the man said. "I noticed as soon as he came in 'cause of the car. I used to have one when I was younger. I was eyeing it, finishing up some stuff at the register to come out and look at it, when this other sweet redone truck pulled up."

"What kind of truck?"

"If I had to guess, I'd say it was a '49 Ford pickup. It was nice too. The job was real good on it."

Zasha bent over him, getting low to his ear, giving Quannah another perfect view. "Keep talking like this and I'll let up a bit. Got it?"

He nodded, eagerly resumed his story, and Zasha released some of the tension in his shoulders.

"It wasn't no rega-lar job either. The inside was done up custom. I wouldn't be surprised if he had a big block engine under that hood the way she purred."

"What color was it?" Quannah asked.

"Alpine blue. It was the original paint color for that model in that year."

Zasha loosened the hold on his arms a little more, and the man's shoulders eased with relief.

"He had all sorts of gadgets pinned to the inside of his driver door like he was James Bond or something."

"Like what?" Quannah prompted.

"A gun, some sort of thing that looked like a cattle prod but wasn't like none I ever seen. And then a medicine in a little glass bottle of some sort that he poured over your friend's head after he zapped him."

"And you believed he was a cop?" Quannah's

tone suggested exactly how unreasonable that conclusion was.

"I did. What else was I supposed to think? I just thought he was some sort of super cop like James Bond."

Quannah bit down on his question of whether the man had ever even seen a Bond movie.

"What else?" Quannah asked.

"Well..." The man looked uncomfortable, and it set Quannah's gut to churning again. "The cop shot your friend first."

Quannah stiffened. "How many times?"

"Three. And they all hit their mark. Looked to be square in the back."

And those bullets were guaranteed to be silver.

"Was my friend alive?"

"Last I saw him, yeah. The cop showed me his badge, 'cause I made him. Then once he told me 'bout how your friend was a fugitive and all, I helped him lift your friend into his truck. He moved the 'Stang to the back, gave me the keys, and took off, saying more criminals might come looking for their friend."

Quannah growled, though it'd do no good. "Is that it?"

"That's it. That's all I know, I swear."

"How long ago did the guy leave?"

"An hour and a half ago? Maybe two."

Far too long for Corin to have silver circulating through his system, and he doubted whoever took him would have taken it out. The "cop" was probably a hunter, which meant an hour and a half to two hours of having Corin was far too long.

"Was my friend conscious when you helped load him into the truck?" Quannah intentionally emphasized the gas station man's role in this. He wasn't off the hook just for being ignorant and content to feed that ignorance, but neither was he fully to blame.

The man shook his head. "No. The cop—or the not-cop—zapped him pretty good with that prod after shooting him up."

And the liquid he poured over Corin's head was probably Wolf Woofer, which would explain why Quannah couldn't reach the alpha.

"You thought it was normal for a cop to shoot, Tase, and pour liquid all over a suspect?" Hayes asked, doing nothing to hold back how pissed off he was at the man on the ground and at the situation.

"I don't argue with cops. I don't wanna be gettin' shot over nothing."

Zasha pressed into his arms, making him wince, just as Quannah would have, just as he wanted to.

"Our friend getting hurt and taken under your watch isn't nothing," Quannah said, the threat riding every one of his syllables. He wouldn't say it, but the man was on his shit list, and he seemed smart enough to know it. No one wanted to be on Quannah's lengthy list.

"Sorry, son," the man said. It was the wrong thing to say.

Quannah stood and met Zasha's waiting eyes. "Let him up."

Once she did, and the man was on his feet, eyes shifty as if he couldn't tell whether they were going to let him go or shoot him, Quannah asked: "Where are the keys to the Mustang?"

"In my pocket."

Quannah held out his hand and the man, with a slight shake to his arm, pulled them out and dropped them in the beta's open palm, careful not to touch him.

Quannah handed them to Roan. "Follow me."

She nodded. "And Zasha?"

"She stays with me," he said, ignoring the rumble that rode his answer.

"What are you going to do to me now?" the man asked, snapping a quick glance at his discarded gun on the ground.

Quannah frowned. "I told you we aren't going to hurt you, but it looks like we are gonna have to tie you up." To Hayes, he said: "Bind him up so he can't get free, and put him somewhere no one will see him. Then lock the place up."

Quannah stared at the gas station attendant for a good half minute before saying, "We'll call the real cops and let them know you're tied up in there in a while. But if you tell them about us…"

The man shook his head so fervently that his thinning white hair bounced around across his scalp. "I won't. I won't tell them nothing."

"Make sure you don't. I don't have reason to come back here ever again, not unless you give me one."

The man swallowed visibly, his Adam's apple bobbing with the action. "You won't need to come back here."

"Good." Then Quannah nodded, Hayes grabbed the man by an arm, and led him inside.

The beta scooped up the shotgun and prepared to put in a quick phone call to the three other cars out searching for Corin. He'd update them, then Flynn, then Chenoa so she could talk to the elders, and finally he'd broadcast to the whole pack.

But quickly. They had to find that truck, and they had to find Corin.

With the whole pack knowing what to look for and what was at stake, their odds of finding him in time ratcheted up to something the beta could live with.

And then the breath swept from Quannah's body as his heart clenched in a painful squeeze. He dropped into a crouch, willing the vertiginous sensation that overwhelmed him to pass.

What was going on?

He reached for his alpha ... and felt nothing.

Even when Corin hadn't answered him before, he'd felt him still there, connected to him through the pack link—just a silent part of it, one he couldn't reach but could almost touch.

Now, there was nothing. Nothing at all.

His lungs swelled, his heart released, and the vertigo abated.

He stood.

Before thinking, he turned toward the she-wolf.

And found Zasha already studying him.

"Did you feel that?" she asked, breathless.

"Feel what?" he asked, voice tight.

It couldn't be...

"I don't know. Like an electric shock or something."

It was just him and her. Roan was already revving up Corin's car. *Kitty* revved so loudly under her touch that it masked the thumping of his heartbeat.

Zasha rubbed at her chest, just beneath the pink, tender flesh. "It's still there. Like it's hooked into me or something."

It couldn't be. It really couldn't.

There was one way to partially confirm.

Flynn, Quannah said. *If you felt anything weird just now, use the pack link to let me know. If nothing odd happened on your end, don't answer.*

Silence pulsed in rhythm with Quannah's beating heart for the next minute.

He stared into Zasha's eyes. The violet of the Smoky Mountain Pack glowed as brightly as a searchlight, overpowering the otherwise bright blue of her irises.

He stared at her.

She stared back.

Quannah reached for the threads that connected him to every single member of their pack—currently, save Corin. Every thread carried the energy of the wolf attached to the other end of it. As if each cord had its own unique scent, he identified hers immediately.

It felt like fire hot enough to burn him. To brand him. To *bond* him.

The link to her vibrated with a strength, resilience, and stubbornness he was beginning to associate just with her.

Down the thread of that link, he asked, just her: *Zasha, can you hear me?*

Her eyes widened until they couldn't widen any more, making the violet streak like flashes of lightning.

Wild just like her.

"Fuck," he said.

And she nodded, her mouth, a sensual temptress, wide open.

THE END...
But only for now!

Smoky Mountain Pack
Book Two
Beta Wolf

Read what happens next with Zasha, Quannah, and Gideon in *Beta Wolf*! It's a wild ride.

BOOKS BY LUCÍA ASHTA

~ FANTASY BOOKS ~

WITCHING WORLD UNIVERSE

Magical Enforcers
Voice of Treason

Magical Dragons Academy
Fae Rider

Smoky Mountain Pack
Forged Wolf
Beta Wolf
Blood Wolf

Witches of Gales Haven

Perfect Pending
Magical Mayhem
Charmed Caper
Pesky Potions

Magical Creatures Academy
Night Shifter
Lion Shifter
Mage Shifter
Power Streak
Power Pendant
Power Shifter
Power Strike

Sirangel
Siren Magic
Angel Magic
Fusion Magic

Magical Arts Academy
First Spell
Winged Pursuit
Unexpected Agents
Improbable Ally
Questionable Rescue
Sorcerers' Web
Ghostly Return

Transformations
Castle's Curse
Spirited Escape
Dragon's Fury
Magic Ignites
Powers Unleashed

Witching World
Magic Awakens
The Five-Petal Knot
The Merqueen
The Ginger Cat
The Scarlet Dragon
Spirit of the Spell
Mermagic

Light Warriors
Beyond Sedona
Beyond Prophecy
Beyond Amber
Beyond Arnaka

PLANET ORIGINS UNIVERSE

Dragon Force
Invisible Born
Invisible Bound

Invisible Rider

Planet Origins
Planet Origins
Original Elements
Holographic Princess
Purple Worlds
Mowab Rider
Planet Sand
Holographic Convergence

OTHER WORLDS

Supernatural Bounty Hunter
(co-authored with Leia Stone)
Magic Bite
Magic Sight
Magic Touch

Pocket Portals
The Orphan Son

STANDALONES

Huntress of the Unseen
A Betrayal of Time
Whispers of Pachamama

BOOKS BY LUCÍA ASHTA

Daughter of the Wind
The Unkillable Killer
Immortalium

~ ROMANCE BOOKS ~

Remembering Him
A Betrayal of Time

ACKNOWLEDGMENTS

I'd write no matter what, because telling stories is a passion, but the following people make creating worlds (and life) a joy. I'm eternally grateful for the support of my beloved, James, my mother, Elsa, and my three daughters, Catia, Sonia, and Nadia. They've always believed in me, even before I published a single word. They help me see the magic in the world around me, and more importantly, within.

I'm thankful for every single one of you who've reached out to tell me that one of my stories touched you in one way or another, made you laugh or cry, or kept you up long past your bedtime. You've given me reason to keep writing.

Finally, thank you to the members of my reader

group. Your constant appreciation of my books helps me show up to write with joy in my heart. And a special beaming smile to Brenda, Miriam, and Aletia for all you do to spread the love for my stories.

ABOUT THE AUTHOR

Lucía Ashta is the Amazon top 100 bestselling author of young adult, new adult, and adult paranormal and urban fantasy books, including the series *Witches of Gales Haven*, *Magical Creatures Academy*, *Sirangel*, *Magical Arts Academy*, *Witching World*, *Dragon Force*, and *Supernatural Bounty Hunter*.

She is also the author of contemporary romance books.

When Lucía isn't writing, she's reading, painting,

or adventuring. Magical fantasy is her favorite, but the romance and quirky characters are what keep her hooked on books.

A former attorney and architect, she's an Argentinian-American author who lives in North Carolina's Smoky Mountains with her beloved and three daughters. She published her first story (about an unusual Cockatoo) at the age of eight, and she's been at it ever since.

Sign up for Lucía's newsletter:
https://www.subscribepage.com/LuciaAshta

Hang out with her:
https://www.facebook.com/groups/LuciaAshta

Connect with her online:
LuciaAshta.com
AuthorLuciaAshta@gmail.com

- facebook.com/authorluciaashta
- bookbub.com/authors/lucia-ashta
- amazon.com/author/luciaashta
- instagram.com/luciaashta

Printed in Great Britain
by Amazon